C000119465

**T.S. Arthur**

# All´s for the Best

# T.S. Arthur

# All´s for the Best

1st Edition | ISBN: 978-3-73406-471-5

Place of Publication: Frankfurt am Main, Germany

Year of Publication: 2019

Outlook Verlag GmbH, Germany.

Reproduction of the original.

# ALL'S FOR THE BEST.

### BY

### T. S. ARTHUR.

PHILADELPHIA:
1869.

# CONTENTS.

# ALL'S FOR THE BEST.

## I.

### FAITH AND PATIENCE.

"*I HAVE* no faith in anything," said a poor doubter, who had trusted in human prudence, and been disappointed; who had endeavored to walk by the lumine of self-derived intelligence, instead of by the light of divine truth, and so lost his way in the world. He was fifty years old! What a sad confession for a man thus far on the journey of life. "No faith in anything."

"You have faith in God, Mr. Fanshaw," replied the gentleman to whom the remark was made.

"In God? I don't know him." And Mr. Fanshaw shook his head, in a

2

bewildered sort of way. There was no levity in his manner. "People talk a great deal about God, and their knowledge of him," he added, but not irreverently. "I think there is often more of pious cant in all this than of living experience. You speak about faith in God. What is the ground of your faith?"

"We have internal sight, as well as external sight."

There was no response to this in Mr. Fanshaw's face.

"We can see with the mind, as well as with the eyes."

"How?"

"An architect sees the building, in all its fine proportions, with the eyes of his mind, before it exists in space visible to his bodily eyes."

"Oh! that is your meaning, friend Wilkins," said Mr. Fanshaw, his countenance brightening a little.

"In part," was replied. "That he can see the building in his mind, establishes the fact of internal sight."

"Admitted; and what then?"

"Admitted, and we pass into a new world—the world of spirit."

Mr. Fanshaw shook his head, and closed his lips tightly.

"I don't believe in spirits," he answered.

"You believe in your own spirit."

"I don't know that I have any spirit."

"You think and feel in a region distinct from the body," said Mr. Wilkins.

"I can't say as to that."

"You can think of justice, of equity, of liberty?"

"Yes."

"As abstract rights; as things essential, and out of the region of simple matter. The body doesn't think; it is the soul."

"Very well. For argument's sake, let all this be granted. I don't wish to cavil. I am in no mood for that. And now, as to the ground of your faith in God."

"Convictions," answered Mr. Wilkins, "are real things to a man. Impressions are one thing; convictions another. The first are like images on a glass; the others like figures in a textile fabric. The first are made in an instant of time, and often pass as quickly; the latter are slowly wrought in the loom of

3

life, through daily experience and careful thought. Herein lies the ground of my faith in God;—it is an inwrought conviction. First I had the child's sweet faith transfused into my soul with a mother's love, and unshadowed by a single doubt. Then, on growing older, as I read the Bible, which I believe to be God's word, I saw that its precepts were divine, and so the child's faith was succeeded by rational sight. Afterwards, as I floated off into the world, and met with storms that wrecked my fondest hopes; with baffling winds and adverse currents; with perils and disappointments, faith wavered sometimes; and sometimes, when the skies were dark and threatening, my mind gave way to doubts. But, always after the storm passed, and the sun came out again, have I found my vessel unharmed, with a freight ready for shipment of value far beyond what I had lost. I have thrown over, in stress of weather, to save myself from being engulfed, things that I had held to be very precious—thrown them over, weeping. But, after awhile, things more precious took their place—goodly pearls, found in a farther voyage, which, but for my loss, would not have been ventured.

"Always am I seeing the hand of Providence—always proving the divine announcement, 'The very hairs of your head are numbered.' Is there not ground for faith here? If the word of God stand in agreement with reason and experience, shall I not have faith? If my convictions are clear, to disbelieve is impossible."

"We started differently," replied Mr. Fanshaw, almost mournfully. "That sweet faith of childhood, to which you have referred, was never mine."

"The faith of manhood is stronger, because it rests on reason and experience," said Mr. Wilkins.

"With me, reason and experience give no faith in God, and no hope in the future. All before me is dark."

"Simply, because you do not use your reason aright, nor read your experiences correctly. If you were to do this, light would fall upon your way. You said, a little while ago, that you had no faith in anything. You spoke without due reflection."

"No; I meant just what I said. Is there stability in anything? In what can I trust to-morrow? simply in nothing. My house may be in ruins—burnt to the ground, at daylight. The friend to whom I loaned my money to-day, to help him in his need, may fail me to-morrow, in my need. The bank in which I hold stock may break—the ship in which I have an adventure, go down at sea. But why enumerate? I am sure of nothing."

"Not even of the love of your child?"

A warm flush came into the face of Mr. Fanshaw. He had one daughter twelve years old.

"Dear Alice!" he murmured, in a softer voice. "Yes, I am sure of that. There is no room for doubt. She loves me."

"One thing in which to have faith," said Mr. Wilkins. "Not in a house which cannot be made wholly safe from fire; nor in a bank, which may fail; nor in a friend's promise; nor in a ship at sea—but in love! Are you afraid to have that love tried? If you were sick or in misfortune, would it grow dim, or perish? Nay, would it not be intensified?

"I think, Mr. Fanshaw," continued his friend, "that you have not tested your faith by higher and better things—by things real and substantial."

"What is more real than a house, or a ship, or a bill of exchange?" asked Mr. Fanshaw.

"Imperishable love—incorruptible integrity—unflinching honor," was replied.

"Do these exist?" Mr. Fanshaw looked incredulous.

"We know that they exist. You know that they exist. History, observation, experience, reason, all come to the proof. We doubt but in the face of conviction. Are these not higher and nobler things than wealth, or worldly honors; than place or power? And is he not serenest and happiest whose life rests on these as a house upon its foundations? You cannot shake such a man. You cannot throw him down. Wealth may go, and friends drop away like withering autumn leaves, but he stands fast, with the light of heaven upon his brow. He has faith in virtue—he has trust in God—he knows that all will come out right in the end, and that he will be a wiser and better man for the trial that tested his principles—for the storms that toughened, but did not break the fibres of his soul."

"You lift me into a new region of thought," said Mr. Fanshaw, "A dim light is breaking into my mind. I see things in a relation not perceived before."

"Will you call with me on an old friend?" asked Mr. Wilkins.

"Who?"

"A poor man. Once rich."

"He might feel my visit as an intrusion."

"No."

"What reduced him to poverty?"

"A friend, in whom he put unlimited faith, deceived and ruined him."

"Ah!"

"And he has never been able to recover himself."

"What is his state of mind?"

"You shall judge for yourself."

In poor lodgings they found a man far past the prime of life. He was in feeble health, and for over two months had not been able to go out and attend to business. His wife was dead, and his children absent. Of all this Mr. Fanshaw had been told on the way. His surprise was real, when he saw, instead of a sad-looking, disappointed and suffering person, a cheerful old man, whose face warmed up on their entrance, as if sunshine were melting over it. Conversation turned in the direction Mr. Wilkins desired it to take, and the question soon came, naturally, from Mr. Fanshaw—

"And pray, sir, how were you sustained amid these losses, and trials, and sorrows?"

"Through faith and patience," was the smiling answer. "Faith in God and the right, and patience to wait."

"But all has gone wrong with you, and kept wrong. The friend who robbed you of an estate holds and enjoys it still; while you are in poverty. He is eating your children's bread."

"Do you envy his enjoyment?" asked the old man.

Mr. Fanshaw shook his head, and answered with an emphasis—"No!"

"I am happier than he is," said the old man. "And as for his eating my children's bread, that is a mistake. His bread is bitter, but theirs is sweet." He reached for a letter that lay on a table near him, and opening it, said—"This is from my son in the West. He writes:—'Dear Father—All is going well with me. I enclose you fifty dollars. In a month I am to be married, and it is all arranged that dear Alice and I shall go East just to see you, and take you back home with us. How nice and comfortable we will make you! And you shall never leave us!'"

The old man's voice broke down on the last sentence, and his eyes filled with tears. But he soon recovered himself, saying—

"Before I lost my property, this son was an idler, and in such danger that through fear of his being led astray, I was often in great distress of mind. Necessity forced him into useful employment; and you see the result. I lost some money, but saved my son. Am I not richer in such love as he bears me to-day, than if, without his love, I possessed a million of dollars? Am I not happier? I knew it would all come out right. I had faith, and I tried to be patient. It is coming out right."

"But the wrong that has been done," said Mr. Fanshaw. "The injustice that exists. Here is a scoundrel, a robber, in the peaceful enjoyment of your goods, while you are in want."

"We do not envy such peace as his. The robber has no peace. He never dwells in security; but is always armed, and on the watch. As for me, it has so turned out that I have never lacked for food and raiment."

"Still, there is the abstract wrong, the evil triumphing over the good," said Mr. Fanshaw.

"How do you reconcile that with your faith in Providence?"

"What I see clearly, as to myself," was replied, "fully justifies the ways of God to man. Am I the gainer or the loser by misfortune? Clearly the gainer. That point admits of no argument. So, what came to me in the guise of evil, I find to be good. God has not mocked my faith in him. I waited patiently until he revealed himself in tender mercy; until the hand to which I clung in the dark valley led me up to the sunny hills. No amount of worldly riches could give me the deep satisfaction I now possess. As for the false friend who robbed me, I leave him in the hands of the all-wise Disposer of events. He will not find, in ill-gotten gain, a blessing. It will not make his bed soft; nor his food sweet to the taste. A just and righteous God will trouble his peace, and make another's possessions the burden of his life."

"But that will not benefit you," said Mr. Fanshaw. "His suffering will not make good your loss."

"My loss is made good already. I have no complaint against Providence. My compensation is a hundredfold. For dross I have gold. I and mine needed the discipline of misfortune, and it came through the perfidy of a friend. That false friend, selfish and grasping—seeing in money the greatest good—was permitted to consummate his evil design. That his evil will punish him, I am sure; and in the pain of his punishment, he may be led to reformation. If he continue to hide the stolen fox, it will tear his vitals. If he lets it go, he will scarcely venture upon a second theft. In either event, the wrong he was permitted to do will be turned into discipline; and my hardest wish in regard to him is, that the discipline may lead to repentance and a better life."

"Your faith and patience," said Mr. Fanshaw, as he held the old man's hand in parting, "rebuke my restless disbelief. I thank you for having opened to my mind a new region of thought—for having made some things clear that have always been dark. I am sure that our meeting to-day is not a simple accident. I have been led here, and for a good purpose."

As Mr. Fanshaw and Mr. Wilkins left the poor man's lodgings, the former said—

"I know the false wretch who ruined your friend."

"Ah!"

"Yes. And he is a miserable man. The fox is indeed tearing his vitals. I understand his case now. He must make restitution. I know how to approach him. This good, patient, trusting old man shall not suffer wrong to the end."

"Does not all this open a new world of thought to your mind?" asked Mr Wilkins. "Does it not show you that, amid all human wrong and disaster, the hand of Providence moves in wise adjustment, and ever out of evil educes good, ever through loss in some lower degree of life brings gain to a higher degree? Consider how, in an unpremeditated way, you are brought into contact with a stranger, and how his life and experience touching yours, give out a spark that lights a candle in your soul to illumine chambers where scarcely a ray had shone before; and this not alone for your benefit. It seems as if you were to be made an instrument of good not only to the wronged, but to the wronger. If you can effect restitution in any degree, the benefit will be mutual."

"I can and I will effect it," replied Mr. Fanshaw. And he did!

## II.

## IS HE A CHRISTIAN?

"*IS* he a Christian?"

The question reached my ear as I sat conversing with a friend, and I paused in the sentence I was uttering, to note the answer.

"Oh, yes; he is a Christian," was replied.

"I am rejoiced to hear you say so. I was not aware of it before," said the other.

"Yes; he has passed from death unto life. Last week, in the joy of his new birth, he united himself to the church, and is now in fellowship with the saints."

"What a blessed change!"

"Blessed, indeed. Another soul saved; another added to the great company of those who have washed their robes, and made them white in the blood of the Lamb. There is joy in heaven on his account."

"Of whom are they speaking?" I asked, turning to my friend.

"Of Fletcher Gray, I believe," was replied.

"Few men stood more in need of Christian graces," said I. "If he is, indeed, numbered with the saints, there is cause for rejoicing."

"By their fruits ye shall know them," responded my friend. "I will believe his claim to the title of Christian, when I see the fruit in good living. If he have truly passed from death unto life, as they say, he will work the works of righteousness. A sweet fountain will not send forth bitter waters."

My friend but expressed my own sentiments in this, and all like cases. I have learned to put small trust in "profession;" to look past the Sunday and prayer-meeting piety of people, and to estimate religious quality by the standard of the Apostle James. There must be genuine love of the neighbor, before there can be a love of God; for neighborly love is the ground in which that higher and purer love takes root. It is all in vain to talk of love as a mere ideal thing. Love is an active principle, and, according to its quality, works. If the love be heavenly, it will show itself in good deeds to the neighbor; but, if infernal, in acts of selfishness that disregard the neighbor.

"I will observe this Mr. Gray," said I, as I walked homeward from the company, "and see whether the report touching him be true. If he is, indeed, a 'Christian,' as they affirm, the Christian graces of meekness and charity will blossom in his life, and make all the air around him fragrant."

Opportunity soon came. Fletcher Gray was a store-keeper, and his life in the world was, consequently, open to the observation of all men. He was likewise a husband and a father. His relations were, therefore, of a character to give, daily, a test of his true quality.

It was only the day after, that I happened to meet Mr. Gray under circumstances favorable to observation. He came into the store of a merchant with whom I was transacting some business, and asked the price of certain goods in the market. I moved aside, and watched him narrowly. There was a marked change in the expression of his countenance and in the tones of his voice. The former had a sober, almost solemn expression; the latter was subdued, even to plaintiveness. But, in a little while, these peculiarities gradually disappeared, and the aforetime Mr. Gray stood there unchanged—unchanged, not only in appearance, but in character. There was nothing of the "yea, yea," and "nay, nay," spirit in his bargain-making, but an eager, wordy effort to gain an advantage in trade. I noticed that, in the face of an asserveration that only five per cent. over cost was asked for a certain article, he still endeavored to procure it at a lower figure than was named by the seller, and finally crowded him down to the exact cost, knowing as he did, that the merchant had a large stock on hand, and could not well afford to hold it over.

"He's a sharper!" said the merchant, turning towards me as Gray left the store.

"He's a Christian, they say," was my quiet remark.

"A Christian!"

"Yes; don't you know that he has become religious, and joined the church?"

"You're joking!"

"Not a word of it. Didn't you observe his subdued, meek aspect, when he came in?"

"Why, yes; now that you refer to it, I do remember a certain peculiarity about him. Become pious! Joined the church! Well, I'm sorry!"

"For what?"

"Sorry for the injury he will do to a good cause. The religion that makes a man a better husband, father, man of business, lawyer, doctor, or preacher, I reverence, for it is genuine, as the lives of those who accept it do testify. But your hypocritical pretenders I scorn and execrate."

"It is, perhaps, almost too strong language, this, as applied to Mr. Gray," said I.

"What is a hypocrite?" asked the merchant.

"A man who puts on the semblance of Christian virtues which he does not possess."

"And that is what Mr. Gray does when he assumes to be religious. A true Christian is just. Was he just to me when he crowded me down in the price of my goods, and robbed me of a living profit, in order that he might secure a double gain? I think not. There is not even the live and let live principle in that. No—no, sir. If he has joined the church, my word for it, there is a black sheep in the fold; or, I might say, without abuse of language, a wolf therein disguised in sheep's clothing."

"Give the man time," said I. "Old habits of life are strong, you know. In a little while, I trust that he will see clearer, and regulate his life from perceptions of higher truths."

"I thought his heart was changed," answered the merchant, with some irony in his tones. "That he had been made a new creature."

I did not care to discuss that point with him, and so merely answered,

"The beginnings of spiritual life are as the beginnings of natural life. The babe is born in feebleness, and we must wait through the periods of infancy, childhood and youth, before we can have the strong man ready for the burden and heat of the day, or full-armed for the battle. If Mr. Gray is in the first effort to lead a Christian life, that is something. He will grow wiser and better in time, I hope."

"There is vast room for improvement," said the merchant. "In my eyes he is, at this time, only a hypocritical pretender. I hope, for the sake of the world and the church both, that his new associates will make something better out of him."

I went away, pretty much of the merchant's opinion. My next meeting with Mr. Gray was in the shop of a mechanic to whom he had sold a bill of goods some months previously. He had called to collect a portion of the amount which remained unpaid. The mechanic was not ready for him.

"I am sorry, Mr. Gray," he began, with some hesitation of manner.

"Sorry for what?" sharply interrupted Mr. Gray.

"Sorry that I have not the money to settle your bill. I have been disappointed——"

"I don't want that old story. You promised to be ready for me to-day, didn't you?" And Mr. Gray knit his brows, and looked angry and imperative.

"Yes, I promised. But——"

"Then keep your promise. No man has a right to break his word. Promises are sacred things, and should be kept religiously."

"If my customers had kept their promises to me there would have been no failure in mine to you," answered the poor mechanic.

"It is of no use to plead other men's failings in justification of your own. You said the bill should be settled to-day, and I calculated upon it. Now, of all things in the world, I hate trifling. I shall not call again, sir!"

"If you were to call forty times, and I hadn't the money to settle your account, you would call in vain," said the mechanic, showing considerable

11

disturbance of mind.

"You needn't add insult to wrong." Mr. Gray's countenance reddened, and he looked angry.

"If there is insult in the case it is on your part, not mine," retorted the mechanic, with more feeling. "I am not a digger of gold out of the earth, nor a coiner of money. I must be paid for my work before I can pay the bills I owe. It was not enough that I told you of the failure of my customers to meet their engagements——"

"You've no business to have such customers," broke in Mr. Gray. "No right to take my goods and sell them to men who are not honest enough to pay their bills."

"One of them is your own son," replied the mechanic, goaded beyond endurance. "His bill is equal to half of yours. I have sent for the amount a great many times, but still he puts me off with excuses. I will send it to you next time."

This was thrusting home with a sharp sword, and the vanquished Mr. Gray retreated from the battle-field, bearing a painful wound.

"That wasn't right in me, I know," said the mechanic, as Gray left his shop. "I'm sorry, now, that I said it. But he pressed me too closely. I am but human."

"He is a hard, exacting, money-loving man," was my remark.

"They tell me he has become a Christian," said the mechanic. "Has got religion—been converted. Is that so?"

"It is commonly reported; but I think common report must be in error. St. Paul gives patience, forbearance, long-suffering, meekness, brotherly kindness, and charity as some of the Christian graces. I do not see them in this man. Therefore, common report must be in error."

"I have paid him a good many hundreds of dollars since I opened my shop here," said the mechanic, with the manner of one who felt hurt. "If I am a poor, hard-working man, I try to be honest. Sometimes I get a little behind hand, as I am new, because people I work for don't pay up as they should. It happened twice before when I wasn't just square with Mr. Gray, and he pressed down very hard upon me, and talked just as you heard him to-day. He got his money, every dollar of it; and he will get his money now. I did think, knowing that he had joined the church and made a profession of religion, that he would bear a little patiently with me this time. That, as he had obtained forgiveness, as alleged, of his sins towards heaven, he would be merciful to his fellow-man. Ah, well! These things make us very sceptical about the honesty of men who call themselves religious. My experience with 'professors' has not been very encouraging. As a general thing I find them quite as greedy for gain as other men. We outside people of the world get to be very sharp-sighted. When a man sets himself up to be of better quality than we, and calls himself by a name significant of heavenly virtue, we judge him, naturally, by his own standard, and watch him very closely. If he remain as hard, as selfish, as exacting, and as eager after money as before, we do not put much faith in his profession, and are very apt to class him with hypocrites. His praying, and fine talk about faith, and heavenly love, and being washed from all sin, excite in us contempt rather than respect. We ask for good works, and are never satisfied with anything else. By their fruits ye shall know them."

On the next Sunday I saw Mr. Gray in church. My eyes were on him when he entered. I noticed that all the lines of his face were drawn down, and that the whole aspect and bearing of the man were solemn and devotional. He moved to his place with a slow step, his eyes cast to the floor. On taking his seat, he leaned his head on the pew in front of him, and continued for nearly a minute in prayer. During the services I heard his voice in the singing; and through the sermon, he maintained the most fixed attention. It was communion Sabbath; and he remained, after the congregation was dismissed, to join in the holiest act of worship.

"Can this man be indeed self-deceived?" I asked myself, as I walked homeward. "Can he really believe that heaven is to be gained by pious acts alone? That every Sabbath evening he can pitch his tent a day's march nearer heaven, though all the week he have failed in the commonest offices of neighborly love?"

It so happened, that I had many opportunities for observing Mr. Gray, who, after joining the church, became an active worker in some of the public and prominent charities of the day. He contributed liberally in many cases, and gave a good deal of time to the prosecution of benevolent enterprises, in which men of some position were concerned. But, when I saw him dispute with a poor gardener who had laid the sods in his yard, about fifty cents, take sixpence off of a weary strawberry woman, or chaffer with his boot-black over an extra shilling, I could not think that it was genuine love for his fellow-men that prompted his ostentatious charities.

In no instance did I find any better estimation of him in business circles; for his religion did not chasten the ardor of his selfish love of advantage in trade; nor make him more generous, nor more inclined to help or befriend the weak and the needy. Twice I saw his action in the case of unhappy debtors, who had not been successful in business. In each case, his claim was among the smallest; but he said more unkind things, and was the hardest to satisfy, of any man among the creditors. He assumed dishonest intention at the outset, and made that a plea for the most rigid exaction; covering his own hard selfishness with offensive cant about mercantile honor, Christian integrity, and religious observance of business contracts. He was the only man among all the creditors, who made his church membership a prominent thing—few of them were even church-goers—and the only man who did not readily make concessions to the poor, down-trodden debtors.

"Is he a Christian?" I asked, as I walked home in some depression of spirits, from the last of these meetings. And I could but answer No—for to be a Christian is to be Christ-like.

"As ye would that men should do to you, do ye even so to them." This is the divine standard. "Ye must be born again," leaves to us no latitude of interpretation. There must be a death of the old, natural, selfish loves, and a new birth of spiritual affections. As a man feels, so will he act. If the affections that rule his heart be divine affections, he will be a lover of others, and a seeker of their good. He will not be a hard, harsh, exacting man in natural things, but kind, forbearing, thoughtful of others, and yielding. In all his dealings with men, his actions will be governed by the heavenly laws of justice and judgment. He will regard the good of his neighbor equally with his own. It is in the world where Christian graces reveal themselves, if they exist at all. Religion is not a mere Sunday affair, but the regulator of a man's conduct among his fellow-men. Unless it does this, it is a false religion, and he who depends upon it for the enjoyment of heavenly felicities in the next life, will find himself in miserable error. Heaven cannot be earned by mere acts of piety, for heaven is the complement of all divine affections in the human soul; and a man must come into these—must be born into them— while on earth, or he can never find an eternal home among the angels of God. Heaven is not gained by doing, but by living.

## III.

## "RICH AND RARE WERE THE GEMS SHE WORE."

"*HAVE* you noticed Miss Harvey's diamonds?" said a friend, directing my attention, as she spoke, to a young lady who stood at the lower end of the room. I looked towards Miss Harvey, and as I did so, my eyes received the sparkle of her gems.

"Brilliant as dew-drops in the morning sunbeams," I remarked.

"Only less brilliant," was my friend's response to this. "Only less brilliant. Nothing holds the sunlight in its bosom so perfectly as a drop of dew.—Next, the diamond. I am told that the pin, now flashing back the light, as it rises and falls with the swell and subsidence of her bosom, cost just one thousand dollars. The public, you know, are very apt to find out the money-value of fine jewelry."

"Miss Harvey is beautiful," said I, "and could afford to depend less on the foreign aid of ornament."

"If she had dazzled us with that splendid pin alone," returned my friend, "we might never have been tempted to look beneath the jewel, far down into the wearer's heart. But, diamond earrings, and a diamond bracelet, added— we know their value to be just twelve hundred dollars; the public is specially inquisitive—suggest some weakness or perversion of feeling, and we become eagle-eyed. But for the blaze of light with which Miss Harvey has surrounded herself, I, for one, should not have been led to observe her closely. There is no object in nature which has not its own peculiar signification; which does not correspond to some quality, affection, or attribute of the mind. This is true of gems; and it is but natural, that we should look for those qualities in the wearer of them to which the gems correspond."

I admitted the proposition, and my friend went on.

"Gold is the most precious of all metals, and it must, therefore, correspond to the most precious attribute, or quality of the mind. What is that attribute?— and what is that quality?"

"Love," said I, after a pause, "Love is the most precious attribute of the mind—goodness the highest quality."

"Then, it is no mere fancy to say that gold corresponds to love, or goodness. It is pure, and ductile, and warm in color, like love; while silver is harder, and white and shining, like truth. Gold and silver in nature are, then, as goodness and truth in the human soul. In one we find the riches of this world, in the other divine riches. And if gold and silver correspond to precious things of the mind, so must brilliant jewels. The diamond! How wonderful is its affection for light—taking in the rays eagerly, dissolving them, and sending them forth again to gladden the eyes in rich prismatic beauty! And to what mental quality must the diamond correspond? As it loves the sun's rays, in which are heat and light—must it not correspond to the affection of things good and true?—heat being of love, and light of truth or wisdom? The wearer of diamonds, then, should have in her heart the heavenly affection to which they correspond. She should be loving and wise."

"It will not do to make an estimate in this way," said I. "The measure is too exacting."

"I will admit that. But we cannot help thinking of the quality when we look upon its sign. With a beautiful face, when first seen, do we not always associate a beautiful soul? And when a lady adorns herself with the most beautiful and costly things in nature, how can we help looking, to see whether they correspond to things in her mind! For one, I cannot; and so, almost involuntarily, I keep turning my eyes upon Miss Harvey, and looking for signs of her quality."

"And how do you read the lady?" I inquired.

My friend shook his head.

"The observation is not favorable."

"Not favorable," he replied. "No, not favorable. She thinks of her jewels—she is vain of them."

"The temptation is great," I said.

"The fact of so loading herself with costly jewels, is in itself indicative of vanity—"

A third party joining us at this moment, we dropped the subject of Miss Harvey. But, enough had been said to make me observe her closely during the evening.

The opening line of Moore's charming lyric,

"Rich and rare were the gems she wore,"

kept chiming in my thoughts, whenever I glanced towards her, and saw the glitter of her diamonds. Yet, past the gems my vision now went, and I searched the fair girl's countenance for the sparkle of other and richer jewels. Did I find them? We shall see.

"Helen," I heard a lady say to Miss Harvey, "is not that Mary Gardiner?"

"I believe so," was her indifferent answer.

"Have you spoken to her this evening?"

"No, aunt."

"Why?"

"Mary Gardiner and I were never very congenial. We have not been thrown together for some time; and now, I do not care to renew the acquaintance."

I obtained a single glance of the young lady's face. It was proud and haughty in expression, and her eyes had in them a cold glitter that awoke in me a feeling of repulsion.

"I wish you were congenial," the lady said, speaking partly to herself.

"We are not, aunt," was Miss Harvey's reply; and she assumed the air of one who felt herself far superior to another with whom she had been brought into comparison.

"The gems do not correspond, I fear," said I to myself, as I moved to another part of the room. "But who is Miss Gardiner?"

In the next moment, I was introduced to the young lady whose name was in my thought. The face into which I looked was of that fine oval which always pleases the eye, even where the countenance itself does not light up well with the changes of thought. But, in this case, a pair of calm, deep, living eyes, and lips of shape most exquisitely delicate and feminine—giving warrant of a beautiful soul—caused the face of Miss Gardiner to hold the vision as by a spell. Low and very musical was her voice, and there was a discrimination in her words, that lifted whatever she said above the commonplace, even though the subjects were of the hour.

I do not remember how long it was after my introduction to Miss Gardiner, before I discovered that her only ornament was a small, exquisitely cut cameo breast-pin, set in a circlet of pearls. There was no obtrusive glitter about this. It lay more like an emblem than a jewel against her bosom. It never drew your attention from her face, nor dimmed, by contrast, the radiance of her soul-lit eyes. I was charmed, from the beginning, with this young lady. Her thoughts were real gems, rich and rare, and when she spoke there was the flash of diamonds in her sentences; not the flash of mere brilliant sayings, like the gleaming of a polished sword, but of living truths, that lit up with their own pure radiance every mind that received them.

Two or three times during the evening, Miss Harvey, radiant in her diamonds—they cost twenty-two hundred dollars—the price would intrude itself—and Miss Gardiner, almost guiltless of foreign ornament, were thrown into immediate contact. But Miss Gardiner was not recognized by the haughty wearer of gems. It was the old farce of pretence, seeking, by borrowed attractions, to outshine the imperishable radiance of truth. I looked on, and read the lesson her conduct gave, and wondered that any were deceived into even a transient admiration. "Rich and rare were the gems she wore," but they

17

had in them no significance as applied to the wearer. It was Miss Gardiner who had the real gems, beautiful as charity, and pure as eternal truth; and she wore them with a simple grace, that charmed every beholder who had eyes clear enough from earthy dust and smoke to see them.

I never meet Miss Harvey, that I do not think of the pure and heavenly things of the mind to which diamonds correspond, nor without seeing some new evidence that she wears no priceless jewels in her soul.

## IV.

## NOT AS A CHILD.

"*I DO* not know how that may be," said the mother, lifting her head, and looking through almost blinding tears, into the face of her friend. "The poet may be right, and, "Not as a child shall I again behold him, but the thought brings no comfort. I have lost my child, and my heart looks eagerly forward to a reunion with him in heaven; to the blessed hour when I shall again hold him in my arms."

"As a babe?"

"Oh, yes. As a darling babe, pure, and beautiful as a cherub."

"But would you have him linger in babyhood forever?" asked the friend.

The mother did not reply.

"Did you expect him always to remain a child here? Would perpetual infancy have satisfied your maternal heart? Had you not already begun to look forward to the period when intellectual manhood would come with its crowning honors?"

"It is true," sighed the mother.

"As it would have been here, so will it be there. Here, the growth of his body would have been parallel, if I may so speak, with the growth of his mind. The natural and the visible would have developed in harmony with the spiritual and the invisible. Your child would have grown to manhood intellectually, as well as bodily. And you would not have had it otherwise. Growth—development—the going on to perfection, are the laws of life; and more emphatically so as appertaining to the life of the human soul. That life, in all its high activities, burns still in the soul of your lost darling, and he will

18

grow, in the world of angelic spirits to which our Father has removed him, up to the full stature of an angel, a glorified form of intelligence and wisdom. He cannot linger in feeble babyhood; in the innocence of simple ignorance; but must advance with the heavenly cycles of changing and renewing states."

"And this is all the comfort you bring to my yearning heart?" said the mother. "My darling, if all you say be true, is lost to me forever."

"He was not yours, but God's." The friend spoke softly, yet with a firm utterance.

"He was mine to love," replied the bereaved one.

"And your love would confer upon its precious object the richest blessings. Dear friend! Lift your thoughts a little way above the clouds that sorrow has gathered around your heart, and let perception come into an atmosphere radiant with light from the Sun of Truth. Think of your child as destined to become, in the better world to which God has removed him, a wise and loving angel. Picture to your imagination the higher happiness, springing from higher capacities and higher uses, which must crown the angelic life. Doing this, and loving your lost darling, I know that you cannot ask for him a perpetual babyhood in heaven."

"I will ask nothing for him but what 'Our Father' pleaseth to give," said the mother, in calmer tones. "My love is selfish, I know. I called that babe mine—mine in the broadest sense—yet he was God's, as every other creature is his—one of the stones in his living temple—one of the members of his kingdom. It does not comfort me in my great sorrow to think that, as a child, I shall not again behold him, but rays of new light are streaming into my mind, and I see things in new aspects and new relations. Out of this deep affliction good will arise."

"Just as certainly," added the friend, "as that the Sun shines and the dew falls. It will be better for you, and better for the child. To both will come a resurrection into higher and purer life."

# V.

## ANGELS IN THE HEART.

*THE* heart is full of guest-chambers that are never empty; and as the heart is the seat of life, these guests are continually acting upon the life, either for good or evil, according to their quality. As the guests are, so our states of life —tranquil and happy, if good; disturbed and miserable, if evil.

We may choose our own guests, if we are wise. None can open the door and come in, unless we give consent; always provided that we keep watch and ward. If we leave wide open the doors of our houses, or neglect to fasten them in the night season, thieves and robbers will enter and despoil us at will. So if we leave the heart, unguarded, enemies will come in. But if we open the door only to good affections—which are guests—then we shall dwell in peace and safety. We have all opened the door for enemies; or let them enter through unguarded portals. They are in all the heart's guest-chambers. They possess the very citadel of life; and the measure of their possession is the measure of our unhappiness.

Markland was an unhappy man; and yet of this world's goods, after which he had striven, he had an abundance. Wealth, honor among men, luxury; these were presented to his mind as things most to be desired, and he reached after them with an ardor that broke down all impediments. Success answered to effort, with almost unerring certainty. So he was full of wealth and honors. But, for all this, Markland was unhappy. There were enemies in the house of his life; troublesome guests in the guest-chambers of his heart, who were forever disturbing, if not wounding him, with their strifes and discords. Some of these he had admitted, himself holding open the door; others had come in by stealth while the entrance was all unguarded.

Envy was one of these guests, and she gave him no peace. He could not bear that another should stand above him in anything. A certain pew in the church he attended was regarded as most desirable. He must have that pew at any cost. So when the annual choice of pews was sold at auction, he overbid all contestants, and secured its occupancy. For all the preceding year, he had failed to enjoy the Sabbath services, because another family had a pew regarded as better situated than his; and now he enjoyed these services as little, through annoyance at having given so large a price for the right of choice, that people smiled when they heard the sum named. He had paid too dear for the privilege, and this fact took away enjoyment.

Envy tormented him in a hundred different ways. He could not enjoy his friend's exquisite statuary, or paintings, because of a secret intimation in his heart that his friend was honored above him in their possession. Twice he had sold almost palatial residences, because their architectural attractions were thrown into the shade by dwellings of later construction. Thousands of dollars each year this troublesome guest cost him; and yet she would never let him be at ease. At every feast of life she dashed his cup with bitterness, and robbed the choicest viands of their zest. He did not enjoy the fame of an author, an orator, an artist, a man of science, a general, or of any who held the world's admiring gaze—for while they stood in the sunlight, he felt cast in the shade. So the guest Envy, warmed and nourished in his heart, proved a tormentor. She gave him neither rest nor peace.

Detraction, twin-sister of Envy, was all the while pointing out defects in friends and neighbors. He saw their faults and hard peculiarities; but rarely their good qualities. Then Doubt and Distrust crept in through the unguarded door, and soon after their entrance Markland began to think uneasily of the future; to fear lest the foundations of worldly prosperity were not sure. These troublesome guests were busiest in the night season, haunting his mind with strange pictures of disasters, and with suggestions touching the arbitrary power of God, whom he feared when the thought of him was present, but did not love. "Whom He will He setteth up, and whom He will He casteth down." Doubt and Distrust revived this warning in his memory, and seeing that it gave his heart a throb of pain, they set it close to his eyes, so that, for a time, he could see nothing else. Thus, night after night, these guests troubled his peace, often driving slumber from his eyelids until the late morning watches. If there had been in his heart that true faith in God which believes in him as doing all things well, Doubt and Distrust might never have gained an entrance. But he had trusted in himself; had believed himself equal to the task of creating his own prosperity—had been, in common phrase, the architect of his own fortunes. And now just as he was pluming himself on success, in crept Doubt and Distrust with their alarming suggestions, and he was unable to cast them out.

Affections, whether evil or good, are social in their character, and obey social laws. They do not like to dwell alone, and therefore seek congenial friendships. They draw to themselves companions of like quality, and are not satisfied until they rule a man as to all the powers of his mind.

In the case of Markland, Envy made room for her twin-sister, Detraction; Ill-will, Jealousy, Unkindness, and a teeming brood of their malevolent kindred crowded into his heart, possessing its chambers, ere a warning reached him of their approach. Is there rest or peace for a man with such guests in his bosom?

Doubt and Distrust only heralded the coming of Fear, Anxiety, Solicitude, Suspicion, Despondency, Foreboding. Markland had only to open his eyes and look around him, to see, on every hand, the unsightly wrecks of palaces once as fair to the eye as that which he had raised with such labor and forethought, and as he contemplated these, Doubt, Distrust, and their companions, filled his mind with alarming thoughts, and so oppressed him with a sense of insecurity that, at times, he saw the advancing shadows of misfortune on his path.

Thus it was with Markland at fifty. He had all good as to the externals of life, yet was he a miserable man, and, worse than all, he felt himself growing more and more unhappy as the years increased. Was there no remedy for this? None, while his heart was so filled with evil affections, which are always tormentors. He did not see this. Though his guests disturbed and afflicted him, he called them friends, and gave them entertainments of the best his house afforded.

Sometimes Pity came to the door of his heart and asked for admission, but he sent Unkindness to double bar it against her. Generosity knocked, but Avarice stood sentinel. Envy was forever refusing to let Good-will, Appreciation, Approval, Delight, come in. Detraction would give no countenance to Virtue and Excellence. Doubt made deadly assault upon Faith, and Trust, and Hope, whenever they drew near, while Ill-will stood ever on the alert to drive off Charity, Loving-kindness and Neighborly regard. Unhappy man! Fiends possessed him, and he knew it not.

It so happened on a time, that Markland, while standing in one of his well-filled ware-houses, saw a child enter and come towards him in a timid, hesitating manner.

"A beggar! Drive her away," said Unkindness and Suspicion, both arousing themselves.

Markland was already lifting his hand to wave her back, when Compassion, who had just then found an old way into his heart, hidden for a long time by rank weeds and brambles, said, in soft and pitying tones:

"She is such a little child!"

"A thieving beggar!" cried Unkindness and Suspicion, angrily.

"A weak little child," pleaded Compassion. "Don't be hard with her. Speak kindly."

Compassion prevailed. Her voice had awakened into life some old and long sleeping memories. Markland was himself, for a moment, a child, full of pity, tenderness and loving-kindness. Compassion had already uncovered the far away past, and the sweetness of its young blossoms was reviving old delights.

"Well, little one, what is wanted?"

Markland hardly knew his own voice, it was so gentle and inviting.

How the pale, pure face of the child warmed and brightened! Gratefully with trust and hope in her eyes, she looked up to the merchant. There was no answer on her lips, for this unexpected kindness had choked the coming utterance. Rebuff, threat, anger, had met her so often, that soft words almost surprised her into tears.

"Well, what can I do for you?"

Compassion held open the door through which she gained an entrance, and already Good-will, Kindness and Satisfaction had come in.

"Mother is sick," said the child.

"A lying vagrant!" exclaimed Suspicion, jarring the merchant's inward ear.

"There is truth in her face," said Compassion, pleading, and, at the same time, she unveiled an image, sharply cut in the past of Markland's life—an image of his own beloved, but long sainted mother, pale and wasted, on her dying bed.

"Give this to your mother," he said, hastily, taking a coin from his pocket. There was more of human kindness in his voice than it had expressed for many years.

"God bless you, sir," the child dropped her grateful eyes from his face, as she took the coin, bending with an involuntary reverent motion. Then, as she slowly passed to the warehouse door, she turned two or three times, to look on the man who, alone, of the many to whom she had made solicitation that day, had answered her in kindness.

"So much for the encouragement of vagrancy," said Suspicion.

"Played on by the art of a cunning child," said Pride.

Markland began to feel ashamed of his momentary weakness. But, he was not now, wholly, at the mercy of the guests who had so long tormented him. Compassion, Good-will and Kindness were now his guests also; and they had other and pleasanter suggestions for his mind. The child's "God bless you, sir," they repeated over and over again, softening the young voice, and giving it increasing power to awaken tender and loving states which had formed themselves in earlier and purer years. Tranquility, so long absent from his soul, came in, now, through the entrance made by Compassion.

Markland went back into his counting-room, almost wondering at the peace he felt. Taking up a newspaper, he read of a rare specimen of statuary just received from Italy, the property of a well-known merchant. Envy did not move quickly enough. The old love of beauty and nature, which envy, detraction, greed of gain, and their blear-eyed companions, had kept in thrall, was already in a freer state; and found in good-will, kindness and tranquility, congenial friends.

So, love of art and beauty ruled his mind in spite of envy, and Markland found real pleasure in the ideal given him by the description he read. It was, almost, a new sensation.

A friend came in, and spoke in praise of one who had performed a generous deed. There was an instant motion among the guests in Markland's heart, the evil inciting to envy and detraction, the good to approval and emulation. Tranquility moved to the door through which she had come in, as if to depart; but Good-will, Kindness and Approbation, drew her back, and held, with her, possession of the mind they sought to rule. Envy and Detraction were shorn, for the time, of their power.

Wondering, as he lay on his bed that night, over the strange peace that pervaded his mind—a peace such as he had not known for many years—Markland fell asleep; and in his sleep there came to him a dream of the human heart and its guest-chamber; and what we have faintly suggested, was made visible to him in living personation.

He saw how evil affections, when permitted to dwell therein, became its enemies and tormentors; and how, just in the degree that kind and good affections gained entrance, there was peace, tranquility and satisfaction.

"I have looked into my own heart," he said, on awaking.

The incident of the child, and the dream that followed, were, in Providence, sent for Markland's instruction. And they were not sent in vain. Ever after he set watch and ward at the doors of his heart. Evil guests, already in possession, were difficult to cast out; but, he invited the good to come in, opening the way by kind and noble acts, done in the face of opposing selfishness. Thus he went on, peopling the guest-chamber with sweet beatitudes, until angels instead of demons filled his house of life.

## VI.

## CAST DOWN, BUT NOT DESTROYED.

"*TRIPPED* again!"

"Who?"

"Brantley."

"Poor fellow! He has a hard time of it. Is he all the way down?"

"I presume so. When he begins to fall, he usually gets to the bottom of the ladder."

It was true; Brantley had tripped again; and was down. He had been climbing bravely for three or four years, and was well up the ladder of prosperity, when in his eagerness to make two rundles of the ladder at a step instead of one, he missed his footing and fell to the bottom. My first knowledge of the fact came through the conversation just recorded. From all I could hear, Brantley's failure was a serious one. I knew him to be honorable and conscientious, and to have a great deal of sensitive pride.

A few days afterwards, while passing the pleasant home where Brantley had been residing, I saw a bill up, giving notice that the house was for sale. A few days later I met him on the street. He did not see me. His eyes were on the pavement; he looked pale and careworn; he walked slowly, and was in deep thought.

"He is of tougher material than most men, if the heart is not all taken out of him," I said in speaking of him to a mutual friend.

"And he *is* of tougher material," was answered, "that is, of finer material. Brantley is not one of your common men."

"Still, there must be something wrong about him. Some defect of judgment. He is a good climber; but not sure-footed. Or, it may be that beyond a certain height his head grows dizzy."

"If one gets too eager in any pursuit, he is almost sure to make false steps. I think Brantley became too eager. The steadily widening prospect as he went up, up, up, caused his pulses to move at a quicker rate."

"Too eager, and less scrupulous," I suggested.

"His honor is unstained," said the friend, with some warmth.

"In the degree that a man grows eager in pursuit, he is apt to grow blind to things collateral, and less concerned about the principles involved."

"In some cases that may be true, but is hardly probable in the case of Brantley. I do not believe that he has swerved from integrity in anything."

"It is my belief," I answered, "that if he had not swerved, he would not have fallen. I may be wrong, but cannot help the impression."

"Brantley is an honest man. I will maintain that in the face of every one," was replied.

"Honest as the world regards honesty. But there are higher than legal standards. What A and B may consider fair, C may regard as questionable. He has his own standard; and if he falls below that in his dealings with men, he departs from his integrity."

"I have nothing to say for Brantley under that view of the subject," said the friend. "If he has special standards of morality, and does not live up to them, the matter is between himself and his own conscience. We, on the outside, are not his judges."

It so happened that I met Brantley a short time afterwards. The circumstances were favorable, and our interview unreserved. He had sold his house, and a large part of the handsome furniture it contained, and was living in a humbler dwelling. I referred to his changed condition, and spoke of it with regret.

"There is no gratuitous evil," he remarked. "I have long been satisfied on that head. If we lose on one hand, we gain on another. And my experience in life leads me to this conclusion, that the loss is generally in lower things, and the gain in higher."

I looked into his face, yet bearing the marks of recent trial and suffering, and saw in it the morning dawn.

"Has it been so with you?" I asked.

"Yes; and it has always been so," he answered, without hesitation. "It is painful to be under the surgeon's knife," he added. "We  shrink back, shivering, at the sight of his instruments. The flesh is agonized. But when all is over, and the greedy tumor, or wasting cancer, that was threatening life, is gone, we rejoice and are glad."

He sighed, and looked sober for a little while, as thought went back, and memory gave too vivid a realization of what had been, and then resumed:

"I can see now, that what seemed to me, and is still regarded by others as a great misfortune, was the best thing that could have taken place. I have lost, but I have gained; and the gain is greater than the loss. It has always been so. Out of every trouble or disaster that has befallen me in life, I have come with a deep conviction that my feet stumbled because they were turning into paths that would lead my soul astray. However much I may love myself and the world, however much I may seek my own, below all and above all is the conviction that time is fleeting, and life here but as a span, that if I compass the whole world, and lose my own soul, I have made a fearful exchange. There are a great many things regarded by business men as allowable. They are so common in trade, that scarcely one man in a score questions their morality; so common, that I have often found myself drifting into  their practice, and abandoning for a time the higher principles in whose guidance there alone is safety. Misfortune seems to have dogged my steps; but in this pause of my life—in this state of calmness—I can see that misfortune is my good; for, not until my feet were turning into ways that lead to death, did I stumble and fall."

"Are you not too hard in self-judgment?" I said.

"No," he answered. "The case stands just here. You know, I presume, the immediate cause of my recent failure in business."

"A sudden decline in stocks."

The color deepened on his cheeks.

"Yes; that is the cause. Now, years ago, I settled it clearly with my own conscience that stock speculation was wrong; that it was only another name for gambling, in which, instead of rendering service to the community, your gains were, in nearly all cases, measured by another's loss. Departing from this just principle of action, I was tempted to invest a large sum of money in a rising stock, that I was sure would continue to advance until it reached a point where, in selling I could realize a net gain of ten thousand dollars. I was doing well. I was putting by from two to three thousand dollars every year, and was in a fair way to get rich. But, as money began to accumulate, I grew more and more eager in its acquirement, and less concerned about the principles underlying every action, until I passed into a temporary state of moral blindness. I was less scrupulous about securing large advantages in trade, and would take the lion's share, if opportunity offered, without a moment's hesitation. So, not content with doing well in a safe path, I must step aside, and try my strength at climbing more rapidly, even though danger threatened on the left and on the right; even though I dragged others down in my hot and perilous scramble upwards. I lost my footing—I stumbled—I fell, crashing down to the very bottom of the hill, half way up which I had gone so safely ere the greedy fiend took possession of me."

"And have not been really hurt by the fall," I remarked.

"I have suffered pain—terrible pain; for I am of a sensitive nature," he replied. "But in the convulsions of agony, nothing but the outside shell of a false life has been torn away. The real man is unharmed. And now that the bitter disappointment and sadness that attend humiliation are over, I can say that my gain is greater than my loss. I would rather grope in the vale of poverty all my life, and keep my conscience clean, than stand high up among the mountains of prosperity with a taint thereon.

"God knows best," he added, after a pause, speaking in a more subdued tone. "And I recognize the hand of His good providence in this wreck of my worldly hopes. To gain riches at the sacrifice of just principles is to gather up dirt and throw away goodly pearls."

"How is it with your family?" I asked. "They must feel the change severely."

"They did feel it. But the pain is over with them also. Poor weak human nature! My girls were active and industrious at home, and diligent at school, while my circumstances were limited. But, as money grew more plentiful, and I gave them a larger house to live in, and richer clothes to wear, they wearied of their useful employments, and neglected their studies. Pride grew apace, and vanity walked hand in hand with pride. They were less considerate of one another, and less loving to their parents. If I attempted to restrain their fondness for dress, or check their extravagance, they grew sullen, or used unfilial language. Like their father, they could not bear prosperity. But all is changed now. Misfortune has restored them to a better state of mind. They emulate each other in service at home; their minds dwell on useful things; they are tender of their mother and considerate of their father. Home is a sweeter place to us all than it has been for a long time."

"And so what the world calls misfortune has proved a blessing."

"Yes. In permitting my feet to stumble; in letting me fall from the height I had obtained, God dealt with me and mine in infinite love. We give false names to things. We call that good which only represents good, which is of the heart and life, and not in external possessions. He has taken from me the effigy that He may give me the good itself."

"If all men could find like you," I said, "a sweet kernel at the centre of misfortune's bitter nut."

"All men may find it if they will," he answered, "for the sweet kernel is there."

How few find it! Nay, reader, if you say this, your observation is at fault. God's providences with men are not like blind chances, but full of wisdom and love. In the darkness of sorrow and adversity a light shines on the path that was not illumined before. When the sun of worldly prosperity goes down, a thousand stars are set in the firmament. In the stillness that follows, God speaks to the soul and is heard.

# VII.

## INTO GOOD GROUND.

"*WHAT* did you think of the sermon, Mr. Braxton?" said one church member to another, as the two men passed from the vestibule of St. Mark's out into the lofty portico.

Mr. Braxton gave a slight shrug, perceived by his companion as a sign of disapproval. They moved along, side by side, down the broad steps to the pavement, closely pressed by the retiring audience.

"Strong meat," said the first speaker, as they got free of the crowd and commenced moving down the street.

"Too strong for my stomach," replied Mr. Braxton. "Something must have gone wrong with our minister when he sat down to write that discourse."

"Indigestion, perhaps."

"Or neuralgia," said Mr. Braxton.

"He was in no amiable mood—that much is certain. Why, he set nine-tenths of us over on the left hand side, among the goats, as remorselessly as if he were an avenging Nemesis. He actually made me shudder."

"That kind of literal application of texts to the living men and women in a congregation is not only in bad taste, but presumptuous and blasphemous. What right has a clergyman to sit in judgment on me, for instance? To give forced constructions to parables and vague generalities in Scripture, about the actual meaning of which divines in all ages have differed; and, pointing his finger to me or to you, say—'The case is yours, sir!' I cannot sit patiently under many more such sermons."

Mr. Braxton evidently spoke from a disturbed state of mind. Something in the discourse had struck at the foundations of self-love and self-complacency.

"Into one ear, and out at the other. So it is with me, in cases like this," answered Mr. Braxton's companion, in a changed and lighter tone. "If a preacher chooses to be savage; to write from dyspeptic or neuralgic states; to send his congregation, unshrived, to the nether regions—why, I shrug my shoulders and let it pass. Most likely, on the next Sunday, he will be full of consideration for tender consciences, and grandly shut the gate he threw open so widely on the last occasion. It would never answer, you know, to take these things to heart—never in the world. We'd always be getting into hot water. Clergymen have their moods, like other people. It doesn't answer to forget this. Good morning, Mr. Braxton. Our ways part here."

"Good morning," was replied, and the men separated.

But, try as Mr. Braxton would to set his minister's closely applied doctrine from Scripture to the account of dyspepsia or neuralgia, he was unable to push from his mind certain convictions wrought therein by the peculiar manner in which some positions had been argued and sustained. The subject taken by the minister, was that striking picture of the judgment given in the twenty-fifth chapter of Matthew, from the thirty-first verse to the close of the chapter, beginning: "When the Son of Man shall come in his glory, and all the holy angels with him, then shall he sit upon the throne of his glory: and before him shall be gathered all nations: and he shall separate them one from another, as a shepherd divideth his sheep from the goats." The passage concludes: "And these shall go away into everlasting punishment: but the righteous into life eternal."

Now, although Mr. Braxton had complained of the literal application of this text, that term was hardly admissible, for the preacher waived the idea of a last general judgment, as involved in the letter of Scripture, and declared his belief in a spiritual signification as lying beneath the letter, and applicable to the inner life of every single individual at the period of departure from this world; adding, in this connection, briefly: "But do not understand me as in any degree waiving the strictness of judgment to which every soul will have to submit. It will not be limited by his acts, but go down to his ends of life— to his motives and his quality—and the sentence will really be a judgment upon what he *is*, not upon what he has *done*; although, taking the barest literal sense, only actions are regarded."

In opening and illustrating his text, he said, farther: "As the word of God, according to its own declarations, is spirit and life—treats, in fact, by virtue of divine and Scriptural origin, of divine and spiritual things, must we not go beneath the merely obvious and natural meaning, if we would get to its true significance? Is there not a hunger of the soul as well as of the body? May we not be spiritually athirst, and strangers?—naked, sick, and in prison? This being so, can we confidently look for the invitation, 'Come, ye blessed of my Father, if our regard for the neighbor have not reached beyond his bodily life? If we have never considered his spiritual wants and sufferings, and ministered thereto according to our ability? Just in the degree that the soul is more precious than the body, is the degree of our responsibility under this more interior signification of Scripture. The mere natural acts of feeding the hungry and giving water to the thirsty, of visiting the sick, and those who lie in prison, of clothing the naked and entertaining strangers, will not save us in our last day, if we have neglected the higher duties involved in the divine admonition. Nor will even the supply of spiritual nourishment to hungry and thirsty souls be accounted to us for righteousness. We must find a higher meaning still in the text. Are we not, each one of us, starving for heavenly food?—spiritually exhausted with thirst?—naked, sick, in prison? Are we eating, daily, of the bread of life?—drinking at the wells of God's truth?—putting on the garments of righteousness?—finding balm for our sick souls in Gilead?—breaking the bonds of evil?—turning from strange lands, and coming back to our father's house. If not, I warn you, men and brethren, that you are not in the right way;—that, taking the significance of God's word, which is truth itself, there is no reasonable ground of hope for your salvation."

It was not with Mr. Braxton as with his friend. He could not let considerations like these enter one ear and go out at the other. From earliest childhood he had received careful instruction. Parents, teachers and preachers, had all shared in the work of storing his mind with the precepts of religion, and now, in manhood, his conscience rested on these and upon the states wrought therefrom in the impressible substance of his mind. Try as he would, he found the effort to push aside early convictions and early impressions a simple impossibility; and, notwithstanding these had been laid on the foundation of a far more literal interpretation of Scripture than the one to which he had just been listening, his maturer reason accepted the preacher's clear application of the law; and conscience, like an angel, went down into his heart, and troubled the waters which had been at peace.

Mr. Braxton was a man of thrift. He had started in life with a purpose, and that purpose he was steadily attaining. To the god of this world he offered daily sacrifice; and in his heart really desired no higher good than seemed attainable through outward things. Wealth, position, honor, among men—these bounded his real aspirations. But prior things in his mind were continually reaching down and affecting his present states. He could not forget that life was short, and earthly possessions and honors but the things of a day. That as he brought nothing into this world, so he could take nothing out. That, without a religious life, he must not hope for heaven. In order to get free from the disturbing influence of these prior things, and to lay the foundations of a future hope, Mr. Braxton became a church member, and, so far as all Sabbath observances were concerned, a devout worshiper. Thus he made a truce with conscience, and conscience having gained so much, accepted for a period the truce, and left Mr. Braxton in good odor with himself.

A man who goes regularly to church, and reads his Bible, cannot fail to have questions and controversies about truths, duties, and the requirements of religion. The barest literal interpretation of Scripture will, in most cases, oppose the action of self-love; and he will not fail to see in the law of spiritual life a requirement wholly in opposition to the law of natural life. In the very breadth of this literal requirement, however, he finds a way of escape from literal observance. To give to all who ask; to lend to all who would borrow; to yield the cloak when the coat is taken forcibly; to turn the left cheek when the right is smitten—all this is to him so evidently but a figure of speech, that he does not find it very hard to satisfy conscience. Setting these passages aside, as not to be taken in the sense of the letter, he does not find it very difficult to dispose of others that come nearer to the obvious duties of man to man— such, for instance, as that in the illustration of which, by the preacher, Mr. Braxton's self-complacency had been so much disturbed. He had never done much in the way of feeding the hungry, giving drink to the thirsty, clothing the naked, or visiting the sick and in prison—never done anything of set purpose, in fact. If people were hungry, it was mostly their own fault, and to feed them would be to encourage idleness and vice. All the other items in the catalogue were as easily disposed of; and so the literal duties involved might have been set forth in the most impassioned eloquence, Sabbath after Sabbath, without much disturbing the fine equipose of Mr. Braxton. Alas for his peace of mind!—the preacher of truth had gone past the dead letter, and revealed its spirit and its life. Suddenly he felt himself removed, as it were, to an almost impossible distance from the heaven into which, as he had complacently flattered himself, he should enter by the door of mere ritual observances, when the sad hour came for giving up the delightful things of this pleasant world. No wonder that Mr. Braxton was disturbed—no wonder that, in his first convictions touching those more interior truths, which made visible the sandy foundations whereon he was building his eternal hopes, he should regard the application of doctrine as personal and even literal.

It was not so easy a thing to set aside the duty of ministering to the hungry, sick, and naked human souls around him, thousands of whom, for lack of spiritual nourishment, medicine and clothing, were in danger of perishing eternally. And the preacher in dwelling upon this great duty of all Christian men and women, had used emphatic language.

"I give you," he said, "God's judgment of the case—not my own. 'Inasmuch as ye did it not unto one of the least of these, ye did it not unto me. And these shall go away;' where? 'To everlasting punishment!' Who shall go thus, in the last day, from this congregation?"

As Mr. Braxton sat alone on the evening of that Sabbath, troubled by the new thoughts which came flowing into his mind, the full impression of this scene in church came back upon him. There was an almost breathless pause. Men leaned forward in their pews; the low, almost whispered, tones of the minister were heard with thrilling distinctness in even the remotest parts of the house.

"Who?" he repeated, and the stillness grew more profound. Then, slowly, impressively, almost sadly, he said:

"I cannot hide the truth. As God's ambassador, I must give the message; and it is this: If you, my brother, are not ministering to the wants of the hungry and thirsty, the stranger, the sick and in prison, you are of those who will have to go away."

And the minister shut the Book, and sat down. If, as we have intimated, the preacher had limited Christian duty to bodily needs, Mr. Braxton would not have been much exercised in mind.

He had found an easy way to dispose of these merely literal interpretations of Scripture. Now, his life was brought to the judgment of a more interior law, as expounded that day. It was in vain that he endeavored to reject the law; for the more he tried to do this, the clearer it was seen in the light of perceptive truth.

"God help me, if this be so!" he exclaimed, in a moment of more perfect realization of what was meant in the Divine Word. "Who shall stand in the judgment?"

For awhile he endeavored to turn himself away from convictions that were grounding themselves deeper and deeper every moment,—to shut his eyes in wilful blindness, and refuse to see in the purer light which had fallen around him. But this effort only brought his mind into severer conflict, and consciously removed him to an almost fatal distance from the paths leading upward to the mountains of peace.

"This is the way, walk ye in it." A clear voice rose above the noise of strife in his soul, and his soul grew calm and listened. He no longer wrought at the fruitless task of rejecting the higher truths which were illustrating his mind, but let them flow in, and by virtue thereof examined the state of his inner life. Now it was that his eyes were in a degree opened, so that he could apprehend the profounder meanings of Scripture. The parables were flooded with new light. He understood, as he had never understood before, why the guest, unclothed with a wedding garment, was cast out from the feast; and why the door was shut upon the virgins who had no oil in their lamps. He had always regarded these parables as involving a hidden meaning—as intended to convey spiritual instruction under literal forms—but, now, they spoke in a language that applied itself to his inward state, and warned him that without a marriage garment, woven in the loom of interior life, where motives rule, he could never be the King's guest; warned him that without the light of divine truth in his understanding, and the oil of love to God and the neighbor in his heart, the door of the kingdom would be shut against him. Ritual observances were, to these, but outward forms, dry husks, except when truly representative of that worship in the soul which subordinates natural affections to what is spiritual and divine.

At last the seed fell into good ground. Mr. Braxton had been a "way-side" hearer; but, ere the good seed had time to germinate, fowls came and devoured it. He had been a "stony-ground" hearer, receiving the truth with gladness, but having no root in himself. He had been as the ground choked with thorns, suffering the cares of this world and the deceitfulness of riches to choke and hinder the growth of heavenly life. Now, into good ground the seed had at last fallen; and though the evil one tried to snatch it away, its hidden life, moving to the earth's quick invitation, was already giving prophetic signs of thirty, sixty, or a hundredfold, in the harvest time.

Why was there good ground in the mind of Mr. Braxton? Good ground, even though he was wedded to external life; a self-seeker; a lover of the world? In the answer to this question lies a most important truth for all to whom God has committed the care of children. Unless good ground is formed, as it was in his case, by early instruction; by storing up in the memory truths from the Bible, and states of good affection; by weaving into the web and woof of the forming mind precepts of religion—there is small hope for the future. If these are not made a part of the forming life, things opposite will be received, and determine spiritual capabilities. Influx of life into the soul must be through prior things; as the twig is bent, the tree is inclined; as the child's memory and consciousness is stored, so will the man develop and progress. Take heart, then, doubting parent; if you have in all faithfulness, woven precious truths, and tender, pious, unselfish states into the texture of your child's mind—though the fruit is not yet seen, depend on it, that the treasured remains of good and true things are there, and will not be lost.

# VIII.

## GIVING THAT DOTH NOT IMPOVERISH.

*OF* all the fallacies accepted by men as truths, there is none more widely prevalent, nor more fatal to happiness, than that which assumes the measure of possession to be the measure of enjoyment. All over the world, the strife for accumulation goes on; every one seeking to increase his flocks and herds —his lands and houses—or his gold and merchandise—and ever in the weary, restless, unsatisfied present, tightening with one hand the grasp on worldly goods, and reaching out for new accessions with the other.

In dispensation, not in possession, lies the secret of enjoyment; a fact which nature illustrates in a thousand ways, and to which every man's experience gives affirmation. "Very good doctrine for the idle and thriftless," said Mr. Henry Steel, a gentleman of large wealth, in answer to a friend, who had advanced the truth we have expressed above.

"As good doctrine for them as for you," was replied. "Possession must come before dispensation. It is not the receiver but the dispenser who gets the higher blessing."

The rich man shrugged his shoulders, and looked slightly annoyed, as one upon whom a distasteful theme was intruded.

"I hear that kind of talk every Sunday," he said, almost impatiently. "But I know what it is worth. Preaching is as much a business as anything else; and this cant about its being more blessed to give than to receive is a part of the capital in trade of your men of black coats and white neck-ties. I understand it all, Mr. Erwin."

"You talk lighter than is your wont on so grave a theme," answered the friend. "What you speak of as 'cant,' and the preacher's 'capital in trade'—'it is more blessed to give than to receive, are the recorded words of him who never spake as man spake. If his words, must they not be true?"

"Perhaps I did speak lightly," was returned. "But indeed, Mr. Erwin, I cannot help feeling that in all these efforts to make rich men believe that their only way to happiness is through a distribution of their estates, a large element of covetousness exists."

"That may be. But, to-day you are worth over a quarter of million of dollars. I remember when fifty thousand, all told, limited the extent of your possessions, and I think you were happier than I find you to-day. How was it, my friend?"

"As to that," was unhesitatingly replied, "I had more true enjoyment in life when I was simply a clerk with a salary of four hundred dollars a year, than I have known at any time since."

"A remarkable confession," said the friend.

"Yet true, nevertheless."

"In all these years of strife with fortune—in all these years of unremitted gain—has there been any great and worthy end in your mind? Any purpose beyond the acquirement of wealth?"

Mr. Steel's brows contracted. He looked at his friend for a moment like one half surprised, and then glanced thoughtfully down at the floor.

"Gain, and only gain," said Mr. Erwin. "Not your history alone, nor mine alone. It is the history of millions. Gathering, gathering, but never of free choice, dispensing. Still, under Providence, the dispensation goes on; and what we hoard, in due time another distributes. Men accumulate gold like water in great reservoirs; accumulate it for themselves, and refuse to lay conduits. Often they pour in their gold until the banks fail under excessive pressure, and the rich treasure escapes to flow back among the people. Often secret conduits are laid, and refreshing and fertilizing currents, unknown to the selfish owner, flow steadily out, while he toils with renewed and anxious labors to keep the repository full. Oftener, the great magazine of accumulated gold and silver, which he never found time to enjoy, is rifled by others at his death. He was the toiler and the accumulator—the slave who only produced. Miners, pearl-divers, gold-washers are we, my friend; but what we gather we fail to possess in that true sense of possession which involves delight and satisfaction. For us the toil, for others the benefit."

"A flattering picture certainly!" was responded by Mr. Steel, with the manner of one on whose mind an unpleasant conviction was forcing itself.

"Is it not true to the life? Death holds out to us his unwelcome hand, and we must leave all. The key of our treasure-house is given, to another."

"Yet, is he not bound by our will?" said Mr. Steel. "As we have ordered, must not he dispense?"

"Why not dispense with our own hands, and with our own eyes see the fruit thereof? Why not, in some small measure, at least prove if it be indeed, more blessed to give than to receive? Let us talk plainly to each other—we are friends. I know that in your will is a bequest of five thousand dollars to a certain charitable institution, that, even in its limited way, is doing much good. I speak now of only this single item. In my will, following your example and suggestion, is a similar bequest of one thousand dollars. You are forty-five and I am forty-seven. How long do we expect to live?"

"Life is uncertain."

"Yet often prolonged to sixty, seventy, or even eighty years. Take sixty-five as the mean. Not for twenty years, then, will this institution receive the benefit of your good intention. It costs, I think, about fifty dollars a year to support each orphan child. Only a small number can be taken, for want of liberal means. Applicants are refused admission almost every day. Three hundred dollars, the interest on five thousand, at six per cent., would pay for six children. Take five years as the average time each would remain in the institution, and we have thirty poor, neglected little ones, taken from the street, and educated for usefulness. Thirty human souls rescued, it may be, from hell, and saved, finally, in heaven. And all this good might be accomplished before your eyes. You might, if you chose, see it in progress, and comprehending its great significance, experience a degree of pleasure, such as fills the hearts of angels. I have made up my mind what to do."

"What?"

"Erase the item of one thousand dollars from my will."

"What then?"

"Call it two thousand, and invest it at once for the use of this charity. No, twenty years shall stand between my purpose and its execution. I will have the satisfaction of knowing that good is done in my lifetime. In this case, at least, I will be my own dispenser."

Love of money was a strong element in the heart of Mr. Steel. The richer he grew, the more absorbing became his desire for riches. It was comparatively an easy thing to write out charitable bequests in a will—to give money for good uses when no longer able to hold possession thereof; but to lessen his valued treasure by taking anything therefrom for others in the present time, was a thing the very suggestion of which startled into life a host of opposing reasons. He did not respond immediately, although his heart moved him to utterance. The force of his friend's argument was, however, conclusive. He saw the whole subject in a new light. After a brief but hard struggle with himself, he answered:

"And I shall follow in your footsteps, my friend. I never thought of the lost time you mention, of the thirty children unblessed by the good act I purposed doing. Can I leave them to vice, to suffering, to crime, and yet be innocent? Will not their souls be required at my hands, now that God shows me their condition? I feel the pressure of a responsibility scarcely thought of an hour ago. You have turned the current of my thoughts in a new direction."

"And what is better still," answered Mr. Erwin, "your purposes also."

"My purposes also," was the reply.

A week afterwards the friends met again.

"Ah," said Mr. Erwin, as he took the hand of Mr. Steel, "I see a new light in your face. Something has taken off from your heart that dead, dull weight of which you complained when I was last here. I don't know when I have seen so cheerful an expression on your countenance."

"Perhaps your eyes were dull before." Mr. Steel's smile was so all-pervading that it lit up every old wrinkle and care-line in his face.

"I was at the school yesterday," said Mr. Erwin, in a meaning way.

"Were you?" The light lay stronger on the speaker's countenance.

"Yes. A little while after you were there."

Mr. Steel took a deep breath, as if his heart had commenced beating more rapidly.

"I have not seen a happier man than the superintendent for a score of weeks. If you had invested the ten thousand dollars for his individual benefit, he could not have been half so well pleased."

"He seems like an excellent man, and one whose heart is in his work," said Mr. Steel.

"He had, already, taken in ten poor little boys and girls on the strength of your liberal donation. Ten children lifted out of want and suffering, and placed under Christian guardianship! Just think of it. My heart gave a leap for joy when he told me. It was well done, my friend—well done!"

"And what of your good purpose, Mr. Erwin?" asked the other.

"Two little girls—babes almost," replied Mr. Erwin, in a lower voice, that almost trembled with feeling, "were brought to me. As I looked at them, the superintendent said: 'I heard of them two days ago. Their wretched mother had just died, and, in dying, had given them to a vicious companion. Hunger, cold, debasement, suffering, crime, were in the way before them; and but for your timely aid, I should have had no power to intervene. But, you gave the means of rescue, and here they are, innocent as yet, and out of danger from the wolf.' In all my life, my friend, there has not been given a moment of sincerer pleasure."

For some time Mr. Steel sat musing.

"This is a new experience," he said, at length. "Something outside of the common order of things. I have made hundreds of investments in my time, but none that paid me down so large an interest. A poor speculation it seemed. You almost dragged me into it; but, I see that it will yield unfailing dividends of pleasure."

"We have turned a leaf in the book of life," his friend made answer, "and on the new page which now lies before us, we find it written, that in wise dispensation, not in mere getting and hoarding, lies the secret of happiness. The lake must have an outlet, and give forth its crystal waters in full measure, if it would keep them pure and wholesome, or, as the Dead Sea, it will be full of bitterness, and hold no life in its bosom."

## IX.

## WAS IT MURDER, OR SUICIDE?

"*WHO* is that young lady?"

A slender girl, just above the medium height, stood a moment at the parlor door, and then withdrew. Her complexion was fair, but colorless; her eyes so dark, that you were in doubt, on the first glance, whether they were brown or blue. Away from her forehead and temples, the chestnut hair was put far back, giving to her finely-cut and regular features an intellectual cast. Her motions were easy, yet with an air of reserve and dignity.

The question was asked by a visitor who had called a little while before.

"My seamstress," answered Mrs. Wykoff.

"Oh!" The manner of her visitor changed. How the whole character of the woman was expressed in the tone with which she made that simple ejaculation! Only a seamstress! "Oh! I thought it some relative or friend of the family."

"No."

"She is a peculiar-looking girl," said Mrs. Lowe, the visitor.

"Do you think so? In what respect?"

"If she were in a different sphere of life, I would say that she had the style of a lady."

"She's a true, good girl," answered Mrs. Wykoff, "and I feel much interested in her. A few years ago her father was in excellent circumstances."

"Ah!" With a slight manifestation of interest.

"Yes, and she's been well educated."

"And has ridden in her own carriage, no doubt. It's the story of two-thirds of your sewing girls." Mrs. Lowe laughed in an unsympathetic, contemptuous way.

"I happen to know that it is true in Mary Carson's case," said Mrs. Wykoff.

"Mary Carson. Is that her name?"

"Yes."

"Passing from her antecedents, as the phrase now is, which are neither here nor there," said Mrs. Lowe, with a coldness, or rather coarseness of manner, that shocked the higher tone of Mrs. Wykoff's feelings, "what is she as a seamstress? Can she fit children?—little girls like my Angela and Grace?"

"I have never been so well suited in my life," replied Mrs. Wykoff. "Let me show you a delaine for Anna which she finished yesterday."

Mrs. Wykoff left the room, and returned in a few minutes with a child's dress in her hand. The ladies examined the work on this dress with practised eyes, and agreed that it was of unusual excellence.

"And she fits as well as she sews?" said Mrs. Lowe.

"Yes. Nothing could fit more beautifully than the dresses she has made for my children."

"How soon will you be done with her?"

"She will be through with my work in a day or two."

"Is she engaged anywhere else?"

"I will ask her, if you desire it."

"Do so, if you please."

"Would you like to see her?"

"It's of no consequence. Say that I will engage her for a couple of weeks. What are her terms?"

"Seventy-five cents a day."

"So much? I've never paid over sixty-two-and-a-half."

"She's worth the difference. I'd rather pay her a dollar a day than give some women I've had, fifty cents. She works faithfully in all things."

"I'll take your word for that, Mrs. Wykoff. Please ask her if she can come to me next week; and if so, on what day?"

Mrs. Wykoff left the room.

"Will Monday suit you?" she asked, on returning.

"Yes; that will do."

"Miss Carson says that she will be at your service on Monday."

"Very well. Tell her to report herself bright and early on that day. I shall be all ready for her."

"Hadn't you better see her, while you are here?" asked Mrs. Wykoff.

"Oh, no. Not at all necessary. It will be time enough on Monday. Your endorsement of her is all-sufficient."

Mrs. Lowe, who had only been making a formal call, now arose, and with a courteous good morning, retired. From the parlor, Mrs. Wykoff returned to the room occupied by Miss Carson.

"You look pale this morning, Mary," said the lady as she came in, "I'm afraid you are not as well as usual."

The seamstress lifted herself in a tired way, and took a long breath, at the same time holding one hand tightly against her left side. Her eyes looked very bright, as they rested, with a sober expression, on Mrs. Wykoff. But she did not reply.

"Have you severe pain there, Mary?" The voice was very kind; almost motherly.

"Not very severe. But it aches in a dull way."

"Hadn't you better lie down for a little while?"

"Oh, no—thank you, Mrs. Wykoff." And a smile flitted over the girl's sweet, sad face; a smile that was meant to say—"How absurd to think of such a thing!" She was there to work, not to be treated as an invalid. Stooping over the garment, she went on with her sewing. Mrs. Wykoff looked at her very earnestly, and saw that her lips were growing colorless; that she moved them in a nervous way, and swallowed every now and then.

"Come, child," she said, in a firm tone, as she took Miss Carson by the arm. "Put aside your work, and lie down on that sofa. You are sick."

She did not resist; but only said—

"Not sick, ma'am—only a little faint."

As her head went heavily down upon the pillow, Mrs. Wykoff saw a sparkle of tears along the line of her closely shut eyelids.

"Now don't stir from there until I come back," said the kind lady, and left the room. In a little while she returned, with a small waiter in her hand, containing a goblet of wine sangaree and a biscuit.

"Take this, Mary. It will do you good."

The eyes which had not been unclosed since Mrs. Wykoff went out, were all wet as Mary Carson opened them.

"Oh, you are so kind!" There was gratitude in her voice. Rising, she took the wine, and drank of it like one athirst. Then taking it from her lips, she sat, as if noting her sensations.

"It seems to put life into me," she said, with a pulse of cheerfulness in her tones.

"Now eat this biscuit," and Mrs. Wykoff held the waiter near.

The wine drank and the biscuit eaten, a complete change in Miss Carson was visible. The whiteness around her mouth gave place to a ruddier tint; her face no longer wore an exhausted air; the glassy lustre of her eyes was gone.

"I feel like myself again," she said, as she left the sofa, and resumed her sewing chair.

"How is your side now?" asked Mrs. Wykoff.

"Easier. I scarcely perceive the pain."

"Hadn't you better lie still a while longer?"

"No, ma'am. I am all right now. A weak spell came over me. I didn't sleep much last night, and that left me exhausted this morning, and without any appetite."

"What kept you awake?"

"This dull pain in my side for a part of the time. Then I coughed a good deal; and then I became wakeful and nervous."

"Does this often occur, Mary?" "Well—

yes, ma'am—pretty often of late." "How

often?"

"Two or three times a week."

"Can you trace it to any cause?"

"Not certainly."

"To cold?"

"No, ma'am."

"Fatigue?"

"More that than anything else, I think."

"And you didn't eat any breakfast this morning?"

"I drank a cup of coffee."

"But took no solid food?"

"I couldn't have swallowed it, ma'am."

"And it's now twelve o'clock," said Mrs. Wykoff, drawing out her watch. "Mary! Mary! This will not do. I don't wonder you were faint just now."

Miss Carson bent to her work and made no answer. Mrs. Wykoff sat regarding her for some time with a look of human interest, and then went out.

A little before two o'clock there was a tap at the door, and the waiter came in, bearing a tray. There was a nicely-cooked chop, toast, and some tea, with fruit and a custard.

"Mrs. Wykoff said, when she went out, that dinner would be late to-day, and that you were not well, and mustn't be kept waiting," remarked the servant, as he drew a small table towards the centre of the room, and covered it with a white napkin.

He came just in time. The stimulating effect of the wine had subsided, and Miss Carson was beginning to grow faint again, for lack of food.

It was after three o'clock when Mrs. Wykoff came home, and half past three before the regular dinner for the family was served. She looked in, a moment, upon the seamstress, saying as she did so—

"You've had your dinner, Mary?"

"Oh yes, ma'am, and I'm much obliged," answered Miss Carson, a bright smile playing over her face. The timely meal had put new life into her.

"I knew you couldn't wait until we were ready," said the kind-hearted, thoughtful woman, "and so told Ellen to cook you a chop, and make you a cup of tea. Did you have enough?"

"Oh yes, ma'am. More than enough."

"You feel better than you did this morning?"

"A great deal better, I'm like another person."

"You must never go without food so long again, Mary. It is little better than suicide for one in your state of health."

Mrs. Wykoff retired, and the seamstress went on with her work.

At the usual hour, Mary Carson appeared on the next morning. Living at some distance from Mrs. Wykoff's, she did not come until after breakfast. The excellent lady had thought over the incident of the day before, and was satisfied that, from lack of nutritious food at the right time, Mary's vital forces were steadily wasting, and that she would, in a very little while, destroy herself.

"I will talk with her seriously about this matter," she said. "A word of admonition may save her."

"You look a great deal better this morning," she remarked, as she entered the room where Mary was sewing.

"I haven't felt better for a long time," was the cheerful answer.

"Did you sleep well last night?"

"Very well."

"Any cough?"

"Not of any consequence, ma'am."

"How was the pain in your side?"

"It troubled me a little when I first went to bed, but soon passed off."

"Did you feel the old exhaustion on waking?"

"I always feel weak in the morning; but it was nothing, this morning, to what it has been."

"How was your appetite?"

"Better. I eat an egg and a piece of toast, and they tasted good. Usually my stomach loathes food in the morning."

"Has this been the case long?"

"For a long time, ma'am."

Mrs. Wykoff mused for a little while, and then asked—

"How do you account for the difference this morning?"

Miss Carson's pale face became slightly flushed, and her eyes fell away from the questioning gaze of Mrs. Wykoff.

"There is a cause for it, and it is of importance that you should know the cause. Has it been suggested to your mind?"

"Yes, ma'am. To me the cause is quite apparent."

They looked at each other for a few moments in silence.

"My interest in you prompts these questions, Mary," said Mrs. Wykoff. "Speak to me freely, if you will, as to a friend. What made the difference?"

"I think the difference is mainly due to your kindness yesterday.—To the glass of wine and biscuit when I was faint, and to the early and good dinner, when exhausted nature was crying for food. I believe, Mrs. Wykoff"—and Mary's eyes glistened—"that if you had not thought of me when you did, I should not be here to-day."

"Are you serious, Mary?"

"I am, indeed, ma'am. I should have got over my faint spell in the morning, even without the wine and biscuit, and worked on until dinner-time; but I wouldn't have been able to eat anything. It almost always happens, when I go so long without food, that my appetite fails altogether, and by the time night comes, I sink down in an exhausted state, from which nature finds it hard to rally. It has been so a number of times. The week before I came here, I was sewing for a lady, and worked from eight o'clock in the morning until four in the afternoon, without food passing my lips. As I had been unable to eat anything at breakfast-time, I grew very faint, and when called to dinner, was unable to swallow a mouthful. When I got home in the evening I was feverish and exhausted, and coughed nearly all night. It was three or four days before I was well enough to go out again."

"Has this happened, in any instance, while you were sewing for me?" asked Mrs. Wykoff.

Miss Carson dropped her face, and turned it partly aside; her manner was slightly disturbed.

"Don't hesitate about answering my question, Mary. If it has happened, say so. I am not always as thoughtful as I should be."

"It happened once."

"When?"

"Last week."

"Oh! I remember that you were not able to come for two days. Now, tell me, Mary, without reservation, exactly how it was."

"I never blamed you for a moment, Mrs. Wykoff. You didn't think; and I'd rather not say anything about it. If I'd been as well as usual on that day, it wouldn't have happened."

"You'd passed a sleepless night?" said Mrs. Wykoff.

"Yes, ma'am."

"The consequence of fatigue and exhaustion?"

"Perhaps that was the reason."

"And couldn't eat any breakfast?"

"I drank a cup of coffee."

"Very well. After that you came here to work. Now, tell me exactly what occurred, and how you felt all day. Don't keep back anything on account of my feelings. I want the exact truth. It will be of use to me, and to others also, I think."

Thus urged, Miss Carson replied—

"I'll tell you just as it was. I came later than usual. The walk is long, and I felt so weak that I couldn't hurry. I thought you looked a little serious when I came in, and concluded that it was in consequence of my being late. The air and walk gave me an appetite, and if I had taken some food then, it would have done me good. I thought, as I stood at the door, waiting to be let in, that I would ask for a cracker or a piece of bread and butter; but, when I met you, and saw how sober you looked, my heart failed me."

"Why, Mary!" said Mrs. Wykoff. "How wrong it was in you!"

"May be it was, ma'am; but I couldn't help it. I'm foolish sometimes; and it's hard for us to be anything else than what we are, as my Aunt Hannah used to say. Well, I sat down to my work with the dull pain in my side, and the sick feeling that always comes at such times, and worked on hour after hour. You looked in once or twice during the morning to see how I was getting on, and to ask about the trimming for a dress I was making. Then you went out shopping, and did not get home until half past two o'clock. For two hours there had been a gnawing at my stomach, and I was faint for something to eat. Twice I got up to ring the bell, and ask for a lunch; but, I felt backward about taking the liberty. When, at three o'clock, I was called to dinner, no appetite remained. I put food into my mouth, but it had no sweetness, and the little I forced myself to swallow, lay undigested. You were very much occupied, and did not notice me particularly. I dragged on, as best I could, through the afternoon, feeling, sometimes, as if I would drop from my chair. You had tea later than usual. It was nearly seven o'clock when I put up my work and went down. You said something in a kind, but absent tone, about my looking pale, and asked if I would have a second cup of tea. I believe I forced myself to eat a slice of bread half as large as my hand. I thought I should never reach home that night, for the weakness that came upon me. I got to bed as soon as possible, but was too tired to sleep until after twelve o'clock, when a coughing spell seized me, which brought on the pain in my side. It was near daylight when I dropped off; and then I slept so heavily for two hours that I was all wet with perspiration when I awoke. On trying to rise, my head swam so that I had to lie down again, and it was late in the day before I could even sit up in bed. Towards evening, I was able to drink a cup of tea and eat a small piece of toast and then I felt wonderfully better. I slept well that night, and was still better in the morning, but did not think it safe to venture out upon a day's work; so I rested and got all the strength I could. On the third day, I was as well as ever again."

Mrs. Wykoff drew a long sigh as Miss Carson stopped speaking and bent down over her sewing. For some time, she remained without speaking.

"Life is too precious a thing to be wasted in this way," said the lady, at length, speaking partly to herself, and partly to the seamstress. "We are too thoughtless, I must own; but you are not blameless. It is scarcely possible for us to understand just how the case stands with one in your position, and duty to yourself demands that you should make it known. There is not one lady in ten, I am sure, who would not be pleased rather than annoyed, to have you do so."

Miss Carson did not answer.

"Do you doubt?" asked Mrs. Wykoff.

"For one of my disposition," was replied, "the life of a seamstress does not take off the keen edge of a natural reserve—or, to speak more correctly sensitiveness. I dislike to break in upon another's household arrangements, or in any way to obtrude myself. My rule is, to adapt myself, as best I can, to the family order, and so not disturb anything by my presence."

"Even though your life be in jeopardy?" said Mrs. Wykoff.

"Oh! it's not so bad as that."

"But it is, Mary! Let me ask a few more questions. I am growing interested in the subject, as reaching beyond you personally. How many families do you work for?"

After thinking for a little while, and naming quite a number of ladies, she replied—

"Not less than twenty."

"And to many of these, you go for only a day or two at a time?"

"Yes."

"Passing from family to family, and adapting yourself to their various home arrangements?"

"Yes, ma'am."

"Getting your dinner at one o'clock to-day, and at three or four to-morrow?"

Miss Carson nodded assent.

"Taking it now, warm and well served, with the family, and on the next occasion, cold and tasteless by yourself, after the family has dined."

Another assenting inclination of the head.

"One day set to work in an orderly, well ventilated room, and on the next cooped up with children in a small apartment, the air of which is little less than poison to your weak lungs."

"These differences must always occur, Mrs. Wykoff," replied Miss Carson, in a quiet uncomplaining voice. "How could it be otherwise? No house-keeper is going to alter her family arrangements for the accommodation of a sewing-girl. The seamstress must adapt herself to them, and do it as gracefully as possible."

"Even at the risk of her life?"

"She will find it easier to decline working in families where the order of things bears too heavily upon her, than to attempt any change. I have been obliged to do this in one or two instances."

"There is something wrong here, Mary," said Mrs. Wykoff, with increasing sobriety of manner. "Something very wrong, and as I look it steadily in the face, I feel both surprise and trouble; for, after what you have just said, I do not see clearly how it is to be remedied. One thing is certain, if you, as a class, accept, without remonstrance, the hurt you suffer, there will be no change. People are indifferent and thoughtless; or worse, too selfish to have any regard for others—especially if they stand, socially, on a plane below them."

"We cannot apply the remedy," answered Miss Carson.

"I am not so sure of that."

"Just look at it for a moment, Mrs. Wykoff. It is admitted, that, for the preservation of health, orderly habits are necessary; and that food should be taken at regular intervals. Suppose that, at home, my habit is to eat breakfast at seven, dinner at one, and supper at six. To-day, such is the order of my meals; but to-morrow, I leave home at half past six, and sit down, on an empty stomach to sew until eight, before I am called to breakfast. After that, I work until two o'clock, when I get my dinner; and at seven drink tea. On the day after that, may be, on my arrival at another house where a day's cutting and fitting is wanted, I find the breakfast awaiting me at seven; this suits very well—but not another mouthful of food passes my lips until after three o'clock, and may be, then, I have such an inward trembling and exhaustion, that I cannot eat. On the day following, the order is again changed. So it goes on. The difference in food, too, is often as great. At some houses, everything is of good quality, well cooked, and in consequence, of easy digestion; while at others, sour or heavy bread, greasy cooking, and like kitchen abominations, if I must so call them, disorder instead of giving sustenance to a frail body like mine. The seamstress who should attempt a change of these things for her own special benefit, would soon find herself in hot water. Think a moment. Suppose, in going into a family for one or two days, or a week, I should begin by a request to have my meals served at certain hours—seven, one and six, for instance—how would it be received in eight out of ten families?"

"Something would depend," said Mrs. Wykoff, "on the way in which it was done. If there was a formal stipulation, or a cold demand, I do not think the response would be a favorable one. But, I am satisfied that, in your case, with the signs of poor health on your countenance, the mild request to be considered as far as practicable, would, in almost every instance, receive a kind return."

"Perhaps so. But, it would make trouble—if no where else, with servants, who never like to do anything out of the common order. I have been living around long enough to understand how such things operate; and generally think it wisest to take what comes and make the best of it."

"Say, rather, the worst of it, Mary. To my thinking, you are making the worst of it."

But, Mrs. Wykoff did not inspire her seamstress with any purpose to act in the line of her suggestions. Her organization was of too sensitive a character to accept the shocks and repulses that she knew would attend, in some quarters, any such intrusion of her individual wants. Even with all the risks upon her, she preferred to suffer whatever might come, rather than ask for consideration. During the two or three days that she remained with Mrs. Wykoff, that excellent lady watched her, and ministered to her actual wants, with all the tender solicitude of a mother; and when she left, tried to impress upon her mind the duty of asking, wherever she might be, for such consideration as her health required.

The Monday morning on which Mary Carson was to appear "bright and early" at the dwelling of Mrs. Lowe, came round, but it was far from being a bright morning. An easterly storm had set in during the night; the rain was falling fast, and the wind driving gustily. A chilliness crept through the frame of Miss Carson as she arose from her bed, soon after the dull light began to creep in drearily through the half closed shutters of her room. The air, even within her chamber, felt cold, damp, and penetrating. From her window a steeple clock was visible. She glanced at the face, and saw that it was nearly seven.

"So late as that!" she exclaimed, in a tone of surprise, and commenced dressing herself in a hurried, nervous way. By the time she was ready to leave her room, she was exhausted by her own excited haste.

"Mary," said a kind voice, calling to her as she was moving down stairs, "you are not going out this morning."

"Oh, yes, ma'am," she answered, in a cheerful voice. "I have an engagement for to-day."

"But the storm is too severe. It's raining and blowing dreadfully. Wait an hour or two until it holds up a little."

"Oh dear, no, Mrs. Grant! I can't stop for a trifle of rain."

"It's no trifle of rain this morning, let me tell you, Mary. You'll get drenched to the skin. Now don't go out, child!"

"I must indeed, Mrs. Grant. The lady expects me, and I cannot disappoint her." And Miss Carson kept on down stairs.

"But you are not going without something on your stomach, Mary. Wait just for a few minutes until I can get you a cup of tea. The water is boiling."

Mary did not wait. It was already past the time when she was expected at Mrs. Lowe's; and besides feeling a little uncomfortable on that account, she had a slight sense of nausea, with its attendant aversion to food. So, breaking away from Mrs. Grant's concerned importunities, she went forth into the cold driving storm. It so happened, that she had to go for nearly the entire distance of six or seven blocks, almost in the teeth of the wind, which blew a gale, drenching her clothes in spite of all efforts to protect herself by means of an umbrella. Her feet and ankles were wet by the time she reached Mrs. Lowe's, and the lower parts of her dress and under-clothing saturated to a depth of ten or twelve inches.

"I expected you half an hour ago," said the lady, in a coldly polite way, as Miss Carson entered her presence.

"The morning was dark and I overslept myself," was the only reply.

Mrs. Lowe did not remark upon the condition of Mary's clothing and feet. That was a matter of no concern to her. It was a seamstress, not a human being, that was before her—a machine, not thing of sensation. So she conducted her to a room in the third story, fronting east, against the cloudy and misty windows of which the wind and rain were driving. There was a damp, chilly feeling in the air of this room. Mrs. Lowe had a knit shawl drawn around her shoulders; but Mary, after removing her bonnet and cloak, had no external protection for her chest beyond the closely fitting body of her merino dress. Her feet and hands felt very cold, and she had that low shuddering, experienced when one is inwardly chilled.

Mrs. Lowe was ready for her seamstress. There were the materials to make half a dozen dresses for Angela and Grace, and one of the little Misses was called immediately, and the work of selecting and cutting a body pattern commenced, Mrs. Lowe herself superintending the operation, and embarrassing Mary at the start with her many suggestions. Nearly an hour had been spent in this way, when the breakfast bell rang. It was after eight o'clock. Without saying anything to Mary, Mrs. Lowe and the child they had been fitting, went down stairs. This hour had been one of nervous excitement to Mary Carson. Her cheeks were hot—burning as if a fire shone upon them —but her cold hands, and wet, colder feet, sent the blood in every returning circle, robbed of warmth to the disturbed heart.

It was past nine o'clock when a servant called Mary to breakfast. As she arose from her chair, she felt a sharp stitch in her left side; so sharp, that she caught her breath in half inspirations, two or three times, before venturing on a full inflation of the lungs. She was, at the same time, conscious of an uncomfortable tightness across the chest. The nausea, and loathing of food, which had given place soon after her arrival at Mrs. Lowe's to a natural craving of the stomach for food, had returned again, and she felt, as she went down stairs, that unless something to tempt the appetite were set before her, she could not take a mouthful. There was nothing to tempt the appetite. The table at which the family had eaten remained just as they had left it—soiled plates and scraps of broken bread and meat; partly emptied cups and saucers; dirty knives and forks, spread about in confusion.—Amid all this, a clean plate had been set for the seamstress; and Mrs. Lowe awaited her, cold and dignified, at the head of the table.

"Coffee or tea, Miss Carson?"

"Coffee."

It was a lukewarm decoction of spent coffee grounds, flavored with tin, and sweetened to nauseousness. Mary took a mouthful and swallowed it—put the cup again to her lips; but they resolutely refused to unclose and admit another drop. So she sat the cup down.

"Help yourself to some of the meat." And Mrs. Lowe pushed the dish, which, nearly three-quarters of an hour before had come upon the table bearing a smoking sirloin, across to the seamstress. Now, lying beside the bone, and cemented to the dish by a stratum of chilled gravy, was the fat, stringy end of the steak. The sight of it was enough for Miss Carson; and she declined the offered delicacy.

"There's bread." She took a slice from a fresh baker's loaf; and spread it with some oily-looking butter that remained on one of the butter plates. It was slightly sour. By forcing herself, she swallowed two or three mouthfuls. But the remonstrating palate would accept no more.

"Isn't the coffee good?" asked Mrs. Lowe, with a sharp quality in her voice, seeing that Miss Carson did not venture upon a second mouthful.

"I have very little appetite this morning," was answered, with an effort to smile and look cheerful.

"Perhaps you'd rather have tea. Shall I give you a cup?" And Mrs. Lowe laid her hand on the teapot.

"You may, if you please." Mary felt an inward weakness that she knew was occasioned by lack of food, and so accepted the offer of tea, in the hope that it might prove more palatable than the coffee. It had the merit of being hot, and not of decidedly offensive flavor; but it was little more in strength than sweetened water, whitened with milk. She drank off the cup, and then left the table, going, with her still wet feet and skirts to the sewing-room.

"Rather a dainty young lady," she heard Mrs. Lowe remark to the waiter, as she left the room.

The stitch in Mary's side caught her again, as she went up stairs, and almost took her breath away; and it was some time after she resumed her work, before she could bear her body up straight on the left side.

In her damp feet and skirts, on a chilly and rainy October day, Mary Carson sat working until nearly three o'clock, without rest or refreshment of any kind; and when at last called to dinner, the disordered condition of the table, and the cold, unpalatable food set before her, extinguished, instead of stimulating her sickly appetite. She made a feint of eating, to avoid attracting attention, and then returned to the sewing-room, the air of which, as she re-entered, seemed colder than that of the hall and dining-room.

The stitch in her side was not so bad during the afternoon; but the dull pain was heavier, and accompanied by a sickening sensation. Still, she worked on, cutting, fitting and sewing with a patience and industry, that, considering her actual condition, was surprising. Mrs. Lowe was in and out of the room frequently, overlooking the work, and marking its progress. Beyond the producing power of her seamstress, she had no thought of that individual. It did not come within the range of her questionings whether she were well or ill

—weak or strong—exhausted by prolonged labor, or in the full possession of bodily vigor. To her, she was simply an agent through which a certain service was obtained; and beyond that service, she was nothing. The extent of her consideration was limited by the progressive creation of dresses for her children. As that went on, her thought dwelt with Miss Carson; but penetrated no deeper. She might be human; might have an individual life full of wants, yearnings, and tender sensibilities; might be conscious of bodily or mental suffering—but, if so, it was in a region so remote from that in which Mrs. Lowe dwelt, that no intelligence thereof reached her.

At six o'clock, Mary put up her work, and, taking her bonnet and shawl, went down stairs, intending to return home.

"You're not going?" said Mrs. Lowe, meeting her on the way. She spoke in some surprise.

"Yes, ma'am. I'm not very well, and wish to get home."

"What time is it?" Mrs. Lowe drew out her watch. "Only six o'clock. I think you're going rather early. It was late when you came this morning, you know."

"Excuse me, if you please," said Miss Carson, as she moved on. "I am not very well to-night. To-morrow I will make it up."

Mrs. Lowe muttered something that was not heard by the seamstress, who kept on down stairs, and left the house.

The rain was still falling and the wind blowing. Mary's feet were quite wet again by the time she reached home.

"How are you, child?" asked Mrs. Grant, in kind concern, as Mary came in.

"Not very well," was answered.

"Oh! I'm sorry! Have you taken cold?"

"I'm afraid that I have."

"I said it was wrong in you to go out this morning. Did you get very wet?"

"Yes."

Mrs. Grant looked down at Mary's feet. "Are they damp?"

"A little."

"Come right into the sitting-room. I've had a fire made up on purpose for you." And the considerate Mrs. Grant hurried Mary into the small back room, and taking off her cloak and bonnet, placed her in a chair before the fire.

Then, as she drew off one of her shoes, and clasped the foot in her hand, she exclaimed—

"Soaking wet, as I live!" Then added, after removing, with kind officiousness, the other shoe—"Hold both feet to the fire, while I run up and get you a pair of dry stockings. Don't take off the wet ones until I come back."

In a few minutes Mrs. Grant returned with the dry stockings and a towel. She bared one of the damp feet, and dried and heated it thoroughly—then warmed one of the stockings and drew it on.

"It feels so good," said Mary, faintly, yet with a tone of satisfaction.

Then the other foot was dried, warmed, and covered. On completing this welcome service, Mrs. Grant looked more steadily into Mary's face, and saw that her cheeks were flushed unnaturally, and that her eyes shone with an unusual lustre. She also noticed, that in breathing there was an effort.

"You got very wet this morning," said Mrs. Grant.

"Yes. The wind blew right in my face all the way. An umbrella was hardly of any use."

"You dried yourself on getting to Mrs. Lowe's?"

Mary shook her head.

"What?"

"There was no fire in the room."

"Why, Mary!"

"I had no change of clothing, and there was no fire in the room. What could I do?"

"You could have gone down into the kitchen, if nowhere else, and dried your feet."

"It would have been better if I had done so; but you know how hard it is for me to intrude myself or give trouble."

"Give trouble! How strangely you do act, sometimes! Isn't life worth a little trouble to save? Mrs. Lowe should have seen to this. Didn't she notice your condition?"

"I think not."

"Well, it's hard to say who deserves most censure, you or she. Such trifling with health and life is a crime. What's the matter?" She observed Mary start as if from sudden pain.

"I have suffered all day, with an occasional sharp stitch in my side—it caught me just then."

Mrs. Grant observed her more closely; while doing so, Mary coughed two or three times. The cough was tight and had a wheezing sound.

"Have you coughed much?" she asked.

"Not a great deal. But I'm very tight here," laying her hand over her breast. "I think," she added, a few moments afterwards, "that I'll go up to my room and get to bed. I feel tired and sick."

"Wait until I can get you some tea," replied Mrs. Grant. "I'll bring down a pillow, and you can lie here on the sofa."

"Thank you, Mrs. Grant. You are so kind and thoughtful." Miss Carson's voice shook a little. The contrast between the day's selfish indifference of Mrs. Lowe, and the evening's motherly consideration of Mrs. Grant, touched her. "I will lie down here for a short time. Perhaps I shall feel better after getting some warm tea. I've been chilly all day."

The pillow and a shawl were brought, and Mrs. Grant covered Mary as she lay upon the sofa; then she went to the kitchen to hurry up tea.

"Come, dear," she said, half an hour afterwards, laying her hand upon the now sleeping girl. A drowsy feeling had come over Mary, and she had fallen into a heavy slumber soon after lying down. The easy touch of Mrs. Grant did not awaken her. So she called louder, and shook the sleeper more vigorously. At this, Mary started up, and looked around in a half-conscious, bewildered manner. Her cheeks were like scarlet.

"Come, dear—tea is ready," said Mrs. Grant.

"Oh! Yes." And Mary, not yet clearly awake, started to leave the room instead of approaching the table.

"Where are you going, child?" Mrs. Grant caught her arm.

Mary stood still, looking at Mrs. Grant, in a confused way.

"Tea is ready." Mrs. Grant spoke slowly and with emphasis.

"Oh! Ah! Yes. I was asleep." Mary drew her hand across her eyes two or three times, and then suffered Mrs. Grant to lead her to the table, where she sat down, leaning forward heavily upon one arm.

"Take some of the toast," said Mrs. Grant, after pouring a cup of tea. Mary helped herself, in a dull way, to a slice of toast, but did not attempt to eat.

Mrs. Grant looked at her narrowly from across the table, and noticed that her eyes, which had appeared large and glittering when she came home, were now lustreless, with the lids drooping heavily.

"Can't you eat anything?" asked Mrs. Grant, in a voice that expressed concern.

Mary pushed her cup and plate away, and leaning back, wearily, in her chair, answered—

"Not just now. I'm completely worn out, and feel hot and oppressed."

Mrs. Grant got up and came around to where Miss Carson was sitting. As she laid her hand upon her forehead, she said, a little anxiously, "You have considerable fever, Mary."

"I shouldn't wonder." And a sudden cough seized her as she spoke. She cried out as the rapid concussions jarred her, and pressed one hand against her side.

"Oh dear! It seemed as if a knife were cutting through me," she said, as the paroxysm subsided, and she leaned her head against Mrs. Grant.

"Come, child," and the kind woman drew upon one of her arms. "In bed is the place for you now."

They went up stairs, and Mary was soon undressed and in bed. As she touched the cool sheets, she shivered for a moment, and then shrank down under the clothes, shutting her eyes, and lying very still.

"How do you feel now?" asked Mrs. Grant, who stood bending over her.

Mary did not reply.

"Does the pain in your side continue?"

"Yes, ma'am." Her voice was dull.

"And the tightness over your breast?"

"Yes, ma'am."

"What can I do for you?"

"Nothing. I want rest and sleep."

Mrs. Grant stood for some time looking down upon Mary's red cheeks; red in clearly defined spots, that made the pale forehead whiter by contrast.

"Something more than sleep is wanted, I fear," she said to herself, as she passed from the chamber and went down stairs. In less than half an hour she returned. A moan reached her ears as she approached the room where the sick girl lay. On entering, she found her sitting high up in bed; or, rather, reclining against the pillows, which she had adjusted against the head-board. Her face, which had lost much of its redness, was pinched and had a distressed look. Her eyes turned anxiously to Mrs. Grant.

"How are you now, Mary?"

"Oh, I'm sick! Very sick, Mrs. Grant."

"Where? How, Mary?"

"Oh, dear!' I'm so distressed here!" laying her hand on her breast. "And every time I draw a breath, such a sharp pain runs through my side into my shoulder. Oh, dear! I feel very sick, Mrs. Grant."

"Shall I send for a doctor?"

"I don't know, ma'am." And Miss Carson threw her head from side to side, uneasily—almost impatiently; then cried out with pain, as she took a deeper inspiration than usual.

Mrs. Grant left the room, and going down stairs, despatched her servant for a physician, who lived not far distant.

"It is pleurisy," said the doctor, on examining the case.—"And a very severe attack," he added, aside, to Mrs. Grant.

Of the particulars of his treatment, we will not speak. He was of the exhaustive school, and took blood freely; striking at the inflammation through a reduction of the vital system. When he left his patient that night, she was free from pain, breathing feebly, and without constriction of the chest. In the morning, he found her with considerable fever, and suffering from a return of the pleuritic pain. Her pulse was low and quick, and had a wiry thrill under the fingers. The doctor had taken blood very freely on the night before, and hesitated a little on the question of opening another vein, or having recourse to cups. As the lancet was at hand, and most easy of use, the vein was opened, and permitted to flow until there was a marked reduction of pain. After this, an anodyne diaphoretic was prescribed, and the doctor retired from the chamber with Mrs. Grant. He was much more particular, now, in his inquiries about his patient and the immediate cause of her illness. On learning that she had been permitted to remain all day in a cold room, with wet feet and damp clothing, he shook his head soberly, and remarked, partly speaking to himself, that doctors were not of much use in suicide or murder cases. Then he asked, abruptly, and with considerable excitement of manner—

"In heaven's name! who permitted this thing to be done? In what family did it occur?"

"The lady for whom she worked yesterday is named Mrs. Lowe."

"Mrs. Lowe!"

"Yes, sir."

"And she permitted that delicate girl to sit in wet clothing, in a room without fire, on a day like yesterday?"

"It is so, doctor."

"Then I call Mrs. Lowe a murderer!" The doctor spoke with excess of feeling.

"Do you think Mary so very ill, doctor?" asked Mrs. Grant.

"I do, ma'am."

"She is free from pain now."

"So she was when I left her last night; and I expected to find her showing marked improvement this morning. But, to my concern, I find her really worse instead of better."

"Worse, doctor? Not worse!"

"I say worse to you, Mrs. Grant, in order that you may know how much depends on careful attendance. Send for the medicine I have prescribed at once, and give it immediately. It will quiet her system and produce sleep. If perspiration follows, we shall be on the right side. I will call in again through the day. If the pain in her side returns, send for me."

The pain did return, and the doctor was summoned. He feared to strike his lancet again; but cupped freely over the right side, thus gaining for the suffering girl a measure of relief. She lay, after this, in a kind of stupor for some hours. On coming out of this, she no longer had the lancinating pain in her side with every expansion of the lungs; but, instead, a dull pain, attended by a cough and tightness of the chest. The cough was, at first, dry, unsatisfactory, and attended with anxiety. Then came a tough mucus, a little streaked with blood. The expectoration soon became freer, and assumed a brownish hue. A low fever accompanied these bad symptoms.

The case had become complicated with pneumonia, and assumed a very dangerous type. On the third day a consulting physician was called in. He noted all the symptoms carefully, and with a seriousness of manner that did not escape the watchful eyes of Mrs. Grant. He passed but few words with the attendant physician, and their exact meaning was veiled by medical terms; but

Mrs. Grant understood enough to satisfy her that little hope of a favorable issue was entertained.

About the time this consultation over the case of Mary Carson was in progress, it happened that Mrs. Wykoff received another visit from Mrs. Lowe.

"I've called," said the latter, speaking in the tone of one who felt annoyed, "to ask where that sewing girl you recommended to me lives?"

"Miss Carson."

"Yes, I believe that is her name."

"Didn't she come on Monday, according to appointment?"

"Oh, yes, she came. But I've seen nothing of her since."

"Ah! Is that so? She may be sick." The voice of Mrs. Wykoff dropped to a shade of seriousness. "Let me see—Monday—didn't it rain?—Yes, now I remember; it was a dreadful day. Perhaps she took cold. She's very delicate. Did she get wet in coming to your house?"

"I'm sure I don't know." There was a slight indication of annoyance on the part of Mrs. Lowe.

"It was impossible, raining and blowing as it did, for her to escape wet feet, if not drenched clothing. Was there fire in the room where she worked?"

"Fire! No. We don't have grates or stoves in any of our rooms."

"Oh; then there was a fire in the heater?"

"We never make fire in the heater before November," answered Mrs. Lowe, with the manner of one who felt annoyed.

Mrs. Wykoff mused for some moments.

"Excuse me," she said, "for asking such minute questions; but I know Miss Carson's extreme delicacy, and I am fearful that she is sick, as the result of a cold. Did you notice her when she came in on Monday morning?"

"Yes. I was standing in the hall when the servant admitted her. She came rather late."

"Did she go immediately to the room where she was to work?"

"Yes."

"You are sure she didn't go into the kitchen and dry her feet?"

"She went up stairs as soon as she came in."

"Did you go up with her?"

"Yes."

"Excuse me, Mrs. Lowe," said Mrs. Wykoff, who saw that these questions were chafing her visitor, "for pressing my inquiries so closely. I am much concerned at the fact of her absence from your house since Monday. Did she change any of her clothing,—take off her stockings, for stance, and put on dry ones?"

"Nothing of the kind."

"But sat in her wet shoes and stockings all day!"

"I don't know that they were wet, Mrs. Wykoff," said the lady, with contracting brows.

"Could you have walked six or seven squares in the face of Monday's driving storm, Mrs. Lowe, and escaped wet feet? Of course not. Your stockings would have been wet half way to the knees, and your skirts also."

There was a growing excitement about Mrs. Wykoff, united with an air of so much seriousness, that Mrs. Lowe began to feel a pressure of alarm. Selfish, cold-hearted and indifferent to all in a social grade beneath her, this lady was not quite ready to stand up in the world's face as one without common humanity. The way in which Mrs. Wykoff was presenting the case of Miss Carson on that stormy morning, did not reflect very creditably upon her; and the thought—"How would this sound, if told of me?"—did not leave her in the most comfortable frame of mind.

"I hope she's not sick. I'm sure the thought of her being wet never crossed my mind. Why didn't she speak of it herself? She knew her own condition, and that there was fire in the kitchen. I declare! some people act in a manner perfectly incomprehensible." Mrs. Lowe spoke now in a disturbed manner.

"Miss Carson should have looked to this herself, and she was wrong in not doing so—very wrong," said Mrs. Wykoff. "But she is shrinking and sensitive to a fault—afraid of giving trouble or intruding herself. *It is our place, I think, when strangers come into our houses, no matter under what circumstances, to assume that they have a natural delicacy about asking for needed consideration, and to see that all things due to them are tendered.* I cannot see that any exceptions to this rule are admissible. To my thinking, it applies to a servant, a seamstress, or a guest, each in a just degree, with equal force. Not that I am blameless in this thing. Far from it. But I acknowledge my fault whenever it is seen, and repenting, resolve to act more humanely in the future."

"Where does Miss Carson live?" asked Mrs. Lowe. "I came to make the inquiry."

"As I feel rather troubled about her," answered Mrs. Wykoff, "I will go to see her this afternoon."

"I wish you would. What you have said makes me feel a little uncomfortable. I hope there is nothing wrong; or, at least, that she is only slightly indisposed. It was thoughtless in me. But I was so much interested in the work she was doing that I never once thought of her personally."

"Did she come before breakfast?"

"Oh, yes."

"Excuse me; but at what time did she get her breakfast?"

There was just a little shrinking in the manner of Mrs. Wykoff; as she answered—

"Towards nine o'clock."

"Did she eat anything?"

"Well, no, not much in particular. I thought her a little dainty. She took coffee; but it didn't just appear to suit her appetite. Then I offered her tea, and she drank a cup."

"But didn't take any solid food?"

"Very little. She struck me as a dainty Miss."

"She is weak and delicate, Mrs. Lowe, as any one who looks into her face may see. Did you give her a lunch towards noon?"

"A lunch! Why no!" Mrs. Lowe elevated her brows.

"How late was it when she took dinner?"

"Three o'clock."

"Did she eat heartily?"

"I didn't notice her particularly. She was at the table for only a few minutes."

"I fear for the worst," said Mrs. Wykoff. "If Mary Carson sat all day on Monday in damp clothes, wet feet, and without taking a sufficient quantity of nourishing food, I wouldn't give much for her life."

Mrs. Lowe gathered her shawl around her, and arose to depart. There was a cloud on her face.

"You will see Miss Carson to-day?" she said.

"Oh, yes."

"At what time do you think of going?"

"I shall not be able to leave home before late in the afternoon."

"Say four o'clock."

"Not earlier than half past four."

Mrs. Lowe stood for some moments with the air of one who hesitated about doing something.

"Will you call for me?" Her voice was slightly depressed.

"Certainly."

"What you have said troubles me. I'm sure I didn't mean to be unkind. It was thoughtlessness altogether. I hope she's not ill."

"I'll leave home at half past four," said Mrs. Wykoff. "It isn't over ten minutes' walk to your house."

"You'll find me all ready. Oh, dear!" and Mrs. Lowe drew a long, sighing breath. "I hope she didn't take cold at my house. I hope nothing serious will grow out of it. I wouldn't have anything of this kind happen for the world. People are so uncharitable. If it should get out, I would be talked about dreadfully; and I'm sure the girl is a great deal more to blame than I am. Why didn't she see to it that her feet and clothes were dried before she sat down to her work?"

Mrs. Wykoff did not answer. Mrs. Lowe stood for a few moments, waiting for some exculpatory suggestion; but Mrs. Wykoff had none to offer.

"Good morning. You'll find me all ready when you call."

"Good morning."

And the ladies parted.

"Ah, Mrs. Lowe! How are you this morning?"

A street meeting, ten minutes later.

"Right well. How are you?"

"Well as usual. I just called at your house."

"Ah, indeed! Come, go back again."

"No, thank you; I've several calls to make this morning. But, d' you know, there's a strange story afloat about a certain lady of your acquaintance?"

"Of my acquaintance?"

"Yes; a lady with whom you are very, very intimate."

"What is it?" There was a little anxiety mixed with the curious air of Mrs. Lowe.

"Something about murdering a sewing-girl."

"What?" Mrs. Lowe started as if she had received a blow; a frightened look came into her face.

"But there isn't anything in it, of course," said the friend, in considerable astonishment at the effect produced on Mrs. Lowe.

"Tell me just what you have heard," said the latter. "You mean me by the lady of your intimate acquaintance."

"Yes; the talk is about you. It came from doctor somebody; I don't know whom. He's attending the girl."

"What is said? I wish to know. Don't keep back anything on account of my feelings. I shall know as to its truth or falsehood; and, true or false, it is better that I should stand fully advised. A seamstress came to work for me on Monday—it was a stormy day, you know—took cold from wet feet, and is now very ill. That much I know. It might have happened at your house, or your neighbors, without legitimate blame lying against either of you. Now, out of this simple fact, what dreadful report is circulated to my injury? As I have just said, don't keep anything back."

"The story," replied the friend, "is that she walked for half a mile before breakfast, in the face of that terrible north-east storm, and came to you with feet soaking and skirts wet to the knees, and that you put her to work, in this condition, in a cold room, and suffered her to sit in her wet garments all day. That, in consequence, she went home sick, was attacked with pleurisy in the evening, which soon ran into acute pneumonia, and that she is now dying. The doctor, who told my friend, called it murder, and said, without hesitation, that you were a murderer."

"Dying! Did he say that she was dying?"

"Yes, ma'am. The doctor said that you might as well have put a pistol ball through her head."

"Me!"

"Yes, you. Those were his words, as repeated by my friend."

"Who is the friend to whom you refer?"

63

"Mrs. T———."

"And, without a word of inquiry as to the degree of blame referable to me, she repeats this wholesale charge, to my injury? Verily, that is Christian charity!"

"I suggested caution on her part, and started to see you at once. Then she did sit in her wet clothing all day at your house?"

"I don't know whether she did or not," replied Mrs. Lowe, fretfully. "She was of woman's age, and competent to take care of herself. If she came in wet, she knew it; and there was fire in the house, at which she could have dried herself. Even a half-witted person, starting from home on a morning like that, and expecting to be absent all day, would have provided herself with dry stockings and slippers for a change. If the girl dies from cold taken on that occasion, it must be set down to suicide, not murder. I may have been thoughtless, but I am not responsible. I'm sorry for her; but I cannot take blame to myself. The same thing might have happened in your house."

"It might have happened in other houses than yours, Mrs. Lowe, I will admit," was replied. "But I do not think it would have happened in mine. I was once a seamstress myself and for nearly two years went out to work in families. What I experienced during those two years has made me considerate towards all who come into my house in that capacity. Many who are compelled to earn a living with the needle, were once in better condition than now, and the change touches some of them rather sharply. In some families they are treated with a thoughtful kindness, in strong contrast with what they receive in other families. If sensitive and retiring, they learn to be very chary about asking for anything beyond what is conceded, and bear, rather than suggest or complain."

"I've no patience with that kind of sensitiveness," replied Mrs. Lowe; "it's simply ridiculous; and not only ridiculous, but wrong. Is every sewing-girl who comes into your house to be treated like an honored guest?"

"We are in no danger of erring, Mrs. Lowe," was answered, "on the side of considerate kindness, even to sewing-women. They are human, and have wants, and weaknesses, and bodily conditions that as imperatively demand a timely and just regard as those of the most honored guest who may sojourn with us. And what is more, as I hold, we cannot omit our duty either to the one or to the other, and be blameless. But I must hurry on. Good morning, Mrs. Lowe."

"Good morning," was coldly responded. And the two ladies parted.

We advance the time a few hours. It is nearly sundown, and the slant beams are coming in through the partly-raised blinds, and falling on the bed, where, white, and panting for the shortcoming breath, lies Mary Carson, a little raised by pillows against which her head rests motionless. Her eyes are shut, the brown lashes lying in two deep fringes on her cheeks. Away from her temples and forehead the hair has been smoothly brushed by loving hands, and there is a spiritual beauty in her face that is suggestive of heaven. Mrs. Grant is on one side of the bed, and the physician on the other. Both are gazing intently on the sick girl's face. The door opens, and two ladies come in, noiselessly—Mrs. Lowe and Mrs. Wykoff. They are strangers there to all but Mary Carson, and she has passed too far on the journey homeward for mortal recognitions. Mrs. Grant moves a little back from the bed, and the two ladies stand in her place, leaning forward, with half-suspended breathing. The almost classic beauty of Miss Carson's face; the exquisite cutting of every feature; the purity of its tone—are all at once so apparent to Mrs. Lowe that she gazes down, wonder and admiration mingling with awe and self-accusation.

There is a slight convulsive cough, with a fleeting spasm. The white lips are stained. Mrs. Lowe shudders. The stain is wiped off, and all is still as before. Now the slanting sun rays touch the pillows, close beside the white face, lighting it with a glory that seems not of the earth. They fade, and life fades with them, going out as they recede. With the last pencil of sunbeams passes the soul of Mary Carson.

"It is over!" The physician breathes deeply, and moves backwards from the bed.

"Over with her," he adds, like one impelled by crowding thoughts to untimely utterance. "The bills of mortality will say pneumonia—*it were better written murder.*"

Call it murder, or suicide, as you will; only, fair reader, see to it that responsibility in such a case lies never at your door.

# X.

## THE NURSERY MAID.

*I DID* not feel in a very good humor either with myself or with Polly, my nursery maid. The fact is, Polly had displeased me; and I, while under the influence of rather excited feelings, had rebuked her with a degree of intemperance not exactly becoming in a Christian gentlewoman, or just to a well meaning, though not perfect domestic.

Polly had taken my sharp words without replying. They seemed to stun her. She stood for a few moments, after the vials of my wrath were emptied, her face paler than usual, and her lips almost colorless. Then she turned and walked from my room with a slow but firm step. There was an air of purpose about her, and a manner that puzzled me a little.

The thermometer of my feelings was gradually falling, though not yet reduced very far below fever-heat, when Polly stood again before me. A red spot now burned on each cheek, and her eyes were steady as she let them rest in mine.

"Mrs. Wilkins," said she, firmly, yet respectfully, "I am going to leave when my month is up."

Now, I have my own share of willfulness and impulsive independence. So I answered, without hesitation or reflection,

"Very well, Polly. If you wish to leave, I will look for another to fill your place." And I drew myself up with an air of dignity.

Polly retired as quickly as she came, and I was left alone with my not very agreeable thoughts for companions. Polly had been in my family for nearly four years, in the capacity of nurse and chamber maid. She was capable, faithful, kind in her disposition, and industrious. The children were all attached to her, and her influence over them was good. I had often said to myself in view of Polly's excellent qualities, "She is a treasure!" And, always, the thought of losing her services had been an unpleasant one. Of late, in some things, Polly had failed to give the satisfaction of former times. She was neither so cheerful, nor so thoughtful, nor had she her usual patience with the children. "Her disposition is altering," I said to myself, now and then, in view of this change; "something has spoiled her."

"You have indulged her too much, I suppose," was the reason given by my husband, whenever I ventured to introduce to his notice the shortcomings of Polly. "You are an expert at the business of spoiling domestics."

My good opinion of myself was generally flattered by this estimate of the case; and, as this good opinion strengthened, a feeling of indignation against Polly for her ingratitude, as I was pleased to call it, found a lodging in my heart.

And so the matter had gone on, from small beginnings, until a state of dissatisfaction on the one part, and coldness on the other, had grown up between mistress and maid. I asked no questions of Polly, as to the change in her manner, but made my own inferences, and took, for granted, my own conclusions. I had spoiled her by indulgence—that was clear. As a thing of course, this view was not very favorable to a just and patient estimate of her conduct, whenever it failed to meet my approval.

On the present occasion, she had neglected the performance of certain services, in consequence of which I suffered some small inconvenience, and a great deal of annoyance.

"I don't know what's come over you, Polly," said I to her sharply. "Something has spoiled you outright; and I tell you now, once for all, that you'll have to mend your ways considerably, if you expect to remain much longer in this family."

The language was hard enough, but the manner harder and more offensive. I had never spoken to her before with anything like the severity now used. The result of this intemperance of speech on my part, the reader has seen. Polly gave notice that she would leave, and I accepted the notice. For a short time after the girl retired from my room, I maintained a state of half indignant independence; but, as to being satisfied with myself, that was out of the question. I had lost my temper, and, as is usual in such cases, had been harsh, and it might be, unjust. I was about to lose the services of a domestic, whose good qualities so far overbalanced all defects and shortcomings, that I could hardly hope to supply her place. How could the children give her up? This question came home with a most unpleasant suggestion of consequences. But, as the disturbance of my feelings went on subsiding, and thought grew clearer and clearer, that which most troubled me was a sense of injustice towards Polly. The suggestion came stealing into my mind, that the something wrong about her might involve a great deal more than I had, in a narrow reference of things to my own affairs, imagined. Polly was certainly changed; but, might not the change have its origin in mental conflict or suffering, which entitled her to pity and consideration, instead of blame?

This was a new thought, which in no way tended to increase a feeling of self-approval.

"She is human, like the rest of us," said I, as I sat talking over the matter with myself, "and every human heart has its portion of bitterness. The weak must bear in weakness, as well as the strong in strength; and the light burden rests as painfully on the back that bends in feebleness, as does the heavy one on Atlas-shoulders. We are too apt to regard those who serve us as mere working machines. Rarely do we consider them as possessing like wants and weaknesses, like sympathies and yearnings with ourselves. Anything will do for them. Under any external circumstances, is their duty to be satisfied."

I was wrong in this matter. Nothing was now clearer to me than this. But, how was I to get right? That was the puzzling question. I thought, and thought —looking at the difficulty first on this side, and then on that. No way of escape presented itself, except through some open or implied acknowledgment of wrong; that is, I must have some plain, kind talk with Polly, to begin with, and thus show her, by an entire change of manner, that I was conscious of having spoken to her in a way that was not met by my own self-approval. Pride was not slow in vindicating her own position among the mental powers. She was not willing to see me humble myself to a servant. Polly had given notice that she was going to leave, and if I made concession, she would, at once conclude that I did so meanly, from self-interest, because I wished to retain her services. My naturally independent spirit revolted under this view of the case, but I marshalled some of the better forces of my mind, and took the field bravely on the side of right and duty. For some time the conflict went on; then the better elements of my nature gained the victory.

When the decision was made, I sent a message for Polly. I saw, as she entered my room, that her cheeks no longer burned, and that the fire had died out in her eyes. Her face was pale, and its expression sad, but enduring.

"Polly," said I, kindly, "sit down. I would like to have some talk with you."

The girl seemed taken by surprise. Her face warmed a little, and her eyes, which had been turned aside from mine, looked at me with a glance of inquiry.

"There, Polly"—and I pointed to a chair—"sit down."

She obeyed, but with a weary, patient air, like one whose feelings were painfully oppressed.

"Polly," said I, with kindness and interest in my voice, "has anything troubled you of late?"

Her face flushed and her eyes reddened.

"If there has, Polly, and I can help you in any way, speak to me as a friend. You can trust me."

I was not prepared for the sudden and strong emotion that instantly manifested itself. Her face fell into her hands, and she sobbed out, with a violence that startled me. I waited until she grew calm, and then said, laying a hand kindly upon her as I spoke—

"Polly, you can talk to me as freely as if I were your mother. Speak plainly, and if I can advise you or aid you in any way, be sure that I will do it."

"I don't think you can help me any, ma'am, unless it is to bear my trouble more patiently," she answered, in a subdued way.

"Trouble, child! What trouble? Has anything gone wrong with you?"

The manner in which this inquiry was made, aroused her, and she said quickly and with feeling:

"Wrong with *me*? O no, ma'am!"

"But you are in trouble, Polly."

"Not for myself, ma'am—not for myself," was her earnest reply.

"For whom, then, Polly?"

The girl did not answer for some moments. Then with a long, deep sigh, she said:

"You never saw my brother Tom, ma'am. Oh, he was such a nice boy, and I was so fond of him! He had a hard place where he worked, and they paid him so little that, poor fellow! if I hadn't spent half my wages on him, he'd never have looked fit to be seen among folks. When he was eighteen he seemed to me perfect. He was so good and kind. But—" and the girl's voice almost broke down—"somehow, he began to change after that. I think he fell into bad company. Oh, ma'am! It seemed as if it would have killed me the first time I found that he had been drinking, and was not himself. I cried all night for two or three nights. When we met again I tried to talk with Tom about it, but he wouldn't hear a word, and, for the first time in his life, got angry with his sister.

"It has been going on from bad, to worse ever since, and I've almost given up hope."

"He's several years younger than you are, Polly."

"Yes, ma'am. He was only ten years old when our mother died. I am glad she is dead now, what I've never said before. There were only two of us— Tom and I; and I being nearly six years the oldest, felt like a mother as well as a sister to him. I've never spent much on myself as you know, and never had as good clothes as other girls with my wages. It took nearly everything for Tom. Oh, dear! What is to come of it all? It will kill me, I'm afraid."

A few questions on my part brought out particulars in regard to Polly's brother that satisfy me of his great lapse from virtue and sobriety. He was now past twenty, and from all I could learn, was moving swift-footed along the road to destruction.

There followed a dead silence for some time after all the story was told. What could I say? The case was one in which it seemed that I could offer neither advice nor consolation. But it was in my power to show interest in the girl, and to let her feel that she had my sympathy. She was sitting with her eyes cast down, and a look of sorrow on her pale, thin face—I had not before re-marked the signs of emaciation—that touched me deeply.

"Polly," said I, with as much kindness of tone as I could express, "it is the lot of all to have trouble, and each heart knows its own bitterness. But on some the trouble falls with a weight that seems impossible to be borne. And this is your case. Yet it only seems to be so, for as our day is, so shall our strength be. If you cannot draw your brother away from the dangerous paths in which he is walking, you can pray for him, and the prayer of earnest love will bring your spirit so near to his spirit, that God may be able to influence him for good through this presence of your spirit with his."

Polly looked at me with a light flashing in her face, as if a new hope had dawned upon her heart.

"Oh, ma'am," she said, "I have prayed, and do pray for him daily. But then I think God loves him better than I can love him, and needs none of my prayer in the case. And so a chill falls over me, and everything grows dark and hopeless—for, of myself, I can do nothing."

"Our prayers cannot change the purposes of God towards any one; but God works by means, and our prayers may be the means through which he can help another."

"How? How? Oh, tell me how, Mrs. Wilkins?"

The girl spoke with great eagerness.

I had an important truth to communicate, but how was I to make it clear to her simple mind? I thought for a moment, and then said—

"When we think of others, we see them."

"In our minds?"

"Yes, Polly. We see them with the eyes of our minds, and are also present with them as to our minds, or spirits. Have you hot noticed that on some occasions you suddenly thought of a person, and that in a little while afterwards that person came in?"

"Oh, yes, I've often noticed, and wondered why it should be so."

"Well, the person in coming to see you, or in approaching the place where you were, thought of you so distinctly that she was present to your mind, or spirit, and you saw her with the eyes of your mind. If this be the right explanation, as I believe it is, then, if we think intently of others, and especially if we think with a strong affection, we are present with them so fully that they think of us, and see our forms with the eyes of their spirits. And now, Polly, keeping this in mind, we may see how praying, in tender love for another, may enable God to do him good; for you know that men and angels are co-workers with God in all good. On the wings of our thought and love, angelic spirits, who are present with us in prayer, may pass with us to the object of our tender interest and thus gaining audience, as it were, stir the heart with good impulses. And who can tell how effectual this may be, if of daily act and long continuance?"

I paused to see if I was comprehended. Polly was listening intently, with her eyes upon the floor. She looked up, after a moment, her countenance calmer than before, but bearing so hopeful an aspect that I was touched with wonder.

"I will pray for him morning, noon, and night," she said, "and if, bodily, I cannot be near him, my spirit shall be present with his many times each day. Oh, if I could but draw him back from the evil into which he has fallen!"

"A sister's loving prayer, and the memory of his mother in heaven, will prove, I trust, Polly, too potent for all his enemies. Take courage!"

In the silence that followed this last remark, Polly arose and stood as if there was something yet unsaid in her mind. I understood her, and made the way plain for both of us.

"If I had known of this before, it would have explained to me some things that gave my mind an unfavorable impression. You have not been like yourself for some time past."

"How could I, ma'am?" Polly's voice trembled and her eyes again filled with tears. "I never meant to displease you; but——"

"All is explained," said I, interrupting her. "I see just how it is; and if I have said a word that hurt you, I am sorry for it. No one could have given better satisfaction in a family than you have given."

"I have always tried to do right," murmured the poor girl, sadly.

"I know it, Polly." My tones were encouraging. "And if you will forget the unkind way in which I spoke to you this morning, and let things remain as they were, it may be better for both of us. You are not fit, taking your state of mind as it now is, to go among strangers."

Polly looked at me with gratitude and forgiveness in her wet eyes. There was a motion of reply about her lips, but she did not trust herself to speak.

"Shall it be as it was, Polly?"

"Oh, yes, ma'am! I don't wish to leave you; and particularly, not now. I am not fit, as you say, to go among strangers. But you must bear with me a little; for I can't always keep my thoughts about me."

When Polly retired from my room, I set myself to thinking over what had happened. The lesson went deeply into my heart. Poor girl! what a heavy burden rested upon her weak shoulders. No wonder that she bent under it! No wonder that she was changed! She was no subject for angry reproof; but for pity and forbearance. If she had come short in service, or failed to enter upon her daily tasks with the old cheerfulness, no blame could attach to her, for the defect was of force and not of will.

"Ah," said I, as I pondered the matter, "how little inclined are we to consider those who stand below us in the social scale, or to think of them as having like passions, like weaknesses, like hopes and fears with ourselves. We deal with them too often as if they were mere working machines, and grow impatient if they show signs of pain, weariness, or irritation. We are quick to blame and slow to praise—chary of kind words, but voluble in reproof—holding ourselves superior in station, but not always showing ourselves superior in thoughtfulness, self-control, and kind forbearance. Ah me! Life is a lesson-book, and we turn a new page every day."

## XI.

## MY FATHER.

*I HAVE* a very early recollection of my father as a cheerful man, and of our home as a place full of the heart's warmest sunshine. But the father of my childhood and the father of my more advanced years wore a very different exterior. He had grown silent, thoughtful, abstracted, but not morose. As his children sprang up around him, full of life and hope, he seemed to lose the buoyant spirits of his earlier manhood. I did not observe this at the time, for I had not learned to observe and reflect. Life was a simple state of enjoyment. Trial had not quickened my perceptions, nor suffering taught me an unselfish regard for others.

The home provided by my father was elegant—some would have called it luxurious. On our education and accomplishments no expense was spared. I had the best teachers—and, of course, the most expensive; with none others would I have been satisfied, for I had come naturally to regard myself as on a social equality with the fashionable young friends who were my companions, and who indulged the fashionable vice of depreciating everything that did not come up to a certain acknowledged standard. Yearly I went to Saratoga or Newport with my sisters, and at a cost which I now think of with amazement. Sometimes my mother went with us, but my father never. He was not able to leave his business. Business! How I came to dislike the word! It was always "business" when we asked him to go anywhere with us; "business" hurried him away from his hastily-eaten meals; "business" absorbed all his thoughts, and robbed us of our father.

"I wish father would give up business," I said to my mother one day, "and take some comfort of his life. Mr. Woodward has retired, and is now living on his income."

My mother looked at me strangely and sighed, but answered nothing.

About this time my father showed some inclination to repress our growing disposition to spend money extravagantly in dress. Nothing but hundred-dollar shawl would suit my ideas. Ada White had been presented by her father with a hundred-dollar cashmere, and I did not mean to be put off with anything less.

"Father, I want a hundred dollars," said I to him one morning as he was leaving the house, after eating his light breakfast. He had grown dyspeptic, and had to be careful and sparing in his diet.

"A hundred dollars!" He looked surprised; in fact, I noticed that my request made him start. "What do you want with so much money?"

"I have nothing seasonable to wear," said I, very firmly; "and as I must have a shawl, I might as well get a good one while I am about it. I saw one at Stewart's yesterday that is just the thing. Ada White's father gave her a shawl exactly like it, and you must let me have the money to buy this one. It will last my lifetime."

"A hundred dollars is a large price for a shawl," said my father, in his sober way.

"Oh, dear, no!" was my emphatic answer; "a hundred dollars is a low price for a shawl. Jane Wharton's cost five hundred."

"I'll think about it," said my father, turning from me rather abruptly.

When he came home at dinner-time, I was alone in the parlor, practicing a new piece of music which my fashionable teacher had left me. He was paid three dollars for every lesson. My father smiled as he laid a hundred-dollar bill on the keys of the piano. I started up, and kissing him, said, with the ardor of a pleased girl—

"What a dear good father you are!"

The return was ample. He always seemed most pleased when he could gratify some wish or supply some want of his children. Ah! if we had been less selfish—less exacting!

It was hardly to be expected that my sisters would see me the possessor of a hundred-dollar shawl, and not desire a like addition to their wardrobes.

"I want a hundred dollars," said my sister Jane, on the next morning, as my father was about leaving for his store.

"Can't spare it to-day, my child," I heard him answer, kindly, but firmly.

"Oh, but I must have it," urged my sister.

"I gave you twenty-five dollars only day before yesterday," my father replied to this. "What have you done with that?"

"Spent it for gloves and laces," said Jane, in a light way, as if the sum were of the smallest possible consequence.

"I am not made of money, child." The tone of my father's voice struck me as unusually sober—almost sad. But Jane replied instantly, and with something of reproach and complaint in her tones—"I shouldn't think you were, if you find it so hard to part with a hundred dollars."

"I have a large payment to make to-day"—my father spoke with unusual decision of manner—"and shall need every dollar that I can raise."

"You gave sister a hundred dollars yesterday," said Jane, almost petulantly.

Not a word of reply did my father make. I was looking at him, and saw an expression on his countenance that was new to me—an expression of pain, mingled with fear. He turned away slowly, and in silence left the house.

"Jane," said my mother, addressing her from the stairway, on which she had been standing, "how could you speak so to your father?"

"I have just as good right to a hundred dollar shawl as Anna," replied my sister, in a very undutiful tone. "And what is more, Im going to have one."

"What reason did your father give for refusing your request to-day?" asked my mother.

"Couldn't spare the money! Had a large payment to make! Only an excuse!"

"Stop, my child!" was the quick, firm remark, made with unusual feeling. "Is that the way to speak of so good a father? Of one who has ever been so kindly indulgent? Jane! Jane! You know not what you are saying!"

My sister looked something abashed at this unexpected rebuke, when my mother took occasion to add, with an earnestness of manner that I could not help remarking as singular,

"Your father is troubled about something. Business may not be going on to his satisfaction. Last night I awoke, and found him walking the floor. To my questions he merely answered that he was wakeful. His health is not so good as formerly, and his spirits are low. Don't, let me pray you, do anything to worry him. Say no more about this money, Jane; you will get it whenever it can be spared."

I did not see my father again until tea-time. Occasionally, business engagements pressed upon him so closely that he did not come home at the usual hour for dining. He looked pale—weary—almost haggard.

"Dear father, are you sick?" said I, laying a hand upon him, and gazing earnestly into his countenance.

"I do not feel very well," he replied, partly averting his face, as if he did not wish me to read its expression too closely. "I have had a weary day."

"You must take more recreation," said I. "This excessive devotion to business is destroying your health. Why will you do it, father?"

He merely sighed as he passed onwards, and ascended to his own room. At tea-time I observed that his face was unusually sober. His silence was nothing uncommon, and so that passed without remark from any one.

On the next day Jane received the hundred dollars, which was spent for a shawl like mine. This brought the sunshine back to her face. Her moody looks, I saw, disturbed my father.

From this time, the hand which had ever been ready to supply all our wants real or imaginary, opened less promptly at our demands. My father talked occasionally of retrenchment and economy when some of our extravagant bills came in; but we paid little heed to his remarks on this head. Where could we retrench? In what could we economize? The very idea was absurd. We had nothing that others moving in our circle did not have. Our house and furniture would hardly compare favorably with the houses and furniture of many of our fashionable friends. We dressed no better—indeed, not so well as dozens of our acquaintances. Retrenchment and economy! I remember laughing with my sisters at the words, and wondering with them what could be coming over our father. In a half-amused way, we enumerated the various items of imaginary reform, beginning at the annual summer recreations, and ending with our milliner's bills. In mock seriousness, we proposed to take the places of cook, chambermaid, and waiter, and thus save these items of expense in the family. We had quite a merry time over our fancied reforms.

But our father was serious. Steadily he persisted in what seemed to us a growing penuriousness. Every demand for money seemed to give him a partial shock, and every dollar that came to us was parted with reluctantly. All this was something new; but we thought less than we felt about it. Our father seemed to be getting into a very singular state of mind.

Summer came round—I shall never forget that summer—and we commenced making our annual preparations for Saratoga. Money was, of course, an indispensable prerequisite. I asked for fifty dollars.

"For what purpose?" inquired my father.

"I haven't a single dress fit to appear in away from home," said I.

"Where are you going?" he asked.

I thought the question a strange one, and replied, a little curtly,

"To Saratoga, of course."

"Oh!" It seemed new to him. Then he repeated my words, in a questioning kind of a way, as if his mind were not altogether satisfied on the subject.

"To Saratoga?"

"Yes, sir. To Saratoga. We always go there. We shall close the season at Newport this year."

"Who else is going?" My father's manner was strange. I had never seen him just in the mood he then appeared to be.

"Jane is going, of course; and so is Emily. And we are trying to persuade mother, also. She didn't go last year. Won't you spend a week or two with us? Now do say yes."

My father shook his head at this last proposal, and said, "No, child!" very decidedly.

"Why?" I asked.

"Because I have something of more importance to think about than Saratoga and its fashionable follies."

"Business! business!" said I, impatiently. "It is the Moloch, father, to which you sacrifice every social pleasure, every home delight, every good! Already you have laid health and happiness upon the bloody altars of this false god!"

A few quick flushes went over his pale face, and then its expression became very sad.

"Anna," he said, after a brief silence, during which even my unpracticed eyes could see that an intense struggle was going on in his mind, "Anna, you will have to give up your visit to Saratoga this year."

"Why, father!" It seemed as if my blood were instantly on fire. My face was, of course, all in a glow. I was confounded, and, let me confess it, indignant; it seemed so like a tyrannical outrage.

"It is simply as I say, my daughter." He spoke without visible excitement. "I cannot afford the expense this season, and you will, therefore, all have to remain in the city."

"That's impossible!" said I. "I couldn't live here through the summer."

"*I* manage to live!" There was a tone in my father's voice, as he uttered these simple words, partly to himself, that rebuked me. Yes, he did manage to live, but *how*? Witness his pale face, wasted form, subdued aspect, brooding silence, and habitual abstraction of mind!

"*I* manage to live!" I hear the rebuking words even now—the tones in which they were uttered are in my ears. Dear father! Kind, tender, indulgent, long-suffering, self-denying! Ah, how little were you understood by your thoughtless, selfish children!

"Let my sisters and mother go," said I, a new regard for my father springing up in my heart; "I will remain at home with you."

"Thank you, dear child!" he answered, his voice suddenly veiled with feeling. "But I cannot afford to let any one go this season."

"The girls will be terribly disappointed. They have set their hearts on going," said I.

"I'm sorry," he said. "But necessity knows no law. They will have to make themselves as contented at home as possible."

And he left me, and went away to his all-exacting "business."

When I stated what he had said, my sisters were in a transport of mingled anger and disappointment, and gave utterance to many unkind remarks against our good, indulgent father. As for my oldest sister, she declared that she would go in spite of him, and proposed our visiting the store of a well-known merchant, where we often made purchases, and buying all we wanted, leaving directions to have the bill sent in. But I was now on my father's side, and resolutely opposed all suggestions of disobedience. His manner and words had touched me, causing some scales to drop from my vision, so that I could see in a new light, and perceive things in a new aspect.

We waited past the usual time for my father's coming on that day, and then dined without him. A good deal to our surprise he came home about four o'clock, entering with an unusual quiet manner, and going up to his own room without speaking to any one of the family.

"Was that your father?" We were sitting together, still discussing the question of Saratoga and Newport. It was my mother who asked the question. We had heard the street door open and close, and had also heard footsteps along the passage and up the stairs.

"It is too early for him to come home," I answered.

My mother looked at her watch, and remarked, as a shade of concern flitted over her face,

"It certainly was your father. I cannot be mistaken in his step. What can have brought him home so early? I hope he is not sick." And she arose and went hastily from the room. I followed, for a sudden fear came into my heart.

"Edward! what ails you? Are you sick?" I heard my mother ask, in an alarmed voice, as I came into her room. My father had laid himself across the bed, and his face was concealed by a pillow, into which it was buried deeply.

"Edward! Edward! Husband! What is the matter? Are you ill?"

"Oh, father! dear father!" I cried, adding my voice to my mother's, and bursting into tears. I grasped his hand; it was very cold. I leaned over, and, pressing down the pillow, touched his face. It was cold also, and clammy with perspiration.

"Send James for the doctor, instantly," said my mother.

"No, no—don't." My father partially aroused himself at this, speaking in a thick, unnatural voice.

"Go!" My mother repeated the injunction, and I flew down stairs with the order for James, our waiter, to go in all haste for the family physician. When I returned, my mother, her face wet with tears, was endeavoring to remove some of my father's outer garments. Together we took off his coat, waistcoat and boots, he making no resistance, and appearing to be in partial stupor, as if under the influence of some drug. We chafed his hands and feet, and bathed his face, that wore a deathly aspect, and used all the means in our power to rekindle the failing spark of life. But he seemed to grow less and less conscious of external things every moment.

When the physician came, he had many questions to ask as to the cause of the state in which he found my father. But we could answer none of them. I watched his face intently, noting every varying expression, but saw nothing to inspire confidence. He seemed both troubled and perplexed. Almost his first act was to bleed copiously.

Twice, before the physician came, had my father been inquired for at the door, a thing altogether unusual at that hour of the day. Indeed, his presence in the house at that hour was something which had not occurred within a year.

"A gentleman is in the parlor, and says that he must see Mr. W——," said the waiter, speaking to me in a whisper, soon after the physician's arrival.

"Did you tell him that father was very ill," said I.

"Yes; but he says that he must see him, sick or well."

"Go down and tell him that father is not in a state to be seen by any one."

The waiter returned in a few moments, and beckoned me to the chamber door.

"The man says that he is not going to leave the house until he sees your father. I wish you would go down to him. He acts so strangely."

Without stopping to reflect, I left the apartment, and hurried down to the parlor. I found a man walking the floor in a very excited manner.

"I wish to see Mr. W——," said he, abruptly, and in an imperative way.

"He is very ill, sir," I replied, "and cannot be seen."

"I must see him, sick or well." His manner was excited.

"Impossible, sir."

The door bell rang again at this moment, and with some violence. I paused, and stood listening until the servant answered the summons, while the man strode twice the full length of the parlor.

"I wish to see Mr. W——." It was the voice of a man.

"He is sick," the servant replied.

"Give him my name—Mr. Walton—and say that I must see him for just a moment." And this new visitor came in past the waiter, and entered the parlor.

"Mr. Arnold!" he ejaculated, in evident surprise.

"Humph! This a nice business!" remarked the first visitor, in a rude way, entirely indifferent to my presence or feelings. "A nice business, I must confess!"

"Have you seen Mr. W——?" was inquired.

"No. They say he's sick."

There was an unconcealed doubt in the voice that uttered this.

"Gentlemen," said I, stung into indignant courage, "this is an outrage! What do you mean by it?"

"We wish to see your father," said the last comer, his manner changing, and his voice respectful.

"You have both been told," was my firm reply, "that my father is too ill to be seen."

"It isn't an hour, as I am told, since he left his store," said the first visitor, "and I hardly think his illness has progressed so rapidly up to this time as to make an interview dangerous. We do not wish to be rude or uncourteous, Miss W——, but our business with your father is imperative, and we must see him. I, for one, do not intend leaving the house until I meet him face to face!"

"Will you walk up stairs?" I had the presence of mind and decision to say, and I moved from the parlor into the passage. The men followed, and I led them up to the chamber where our distressed family were gathered around my father. As we entered the hushed apartment the men pressed forward somewhat eagerly, but their steps were suddenly arrested. The sight was one to make its own impression. My father's face, deathly in its hue, was turned towards the door, and from his bared arm a stream of dark blood was flowing sluggishly. The physician had just opened a vein.

"Come! This is no place for us," I heard one of the men whisper to the other, and they withdrew as unceremoniously as they had entered. Scarcely had they gone ere the loud ringing of the door bell sounded through the house again.

"What does all this mean!" whispered my distressed mother.

"I cannot tell. Something is wrong," was all that I could answer; and a vague, terrible fear took possession of my heart.

In the midst of our confusion, uncertainty and distress, my uncle, the only relative of my mother, arrived, and from him we learned the crushing fact that my father's paper had been that day dishonored at bank. In other words, that he had failed in business.

The blow, long suspended over his head; and as I afterwards learned, long dreaded, and long averted by the most desperate expedients to save himself from ruin, when it did fall, was too heavy for him. It crushed the life out of his enfeebled system. That fearful night he died!

It is not my purpose to draw towards the survivors any sympathy, by picturing the changes in their fortunes and modes of life that followed this sad event. They have all endured much and suffered much. But how light has it been to what my father must have endured and suffered in his long struggle to sustain the thoughtless extravagance of his family—to supply them with comforts and luxuries, none of which he could himself enjoy! Ever before me is the image of his gradually wasting form, and pale, sober, anxious face. His voice, always mild, now comes to my ears, in memory, burdened with a most touching sadness. What could we have been thinking about? Oh, youth! how blindly selfish thou art! How unjust in thy thoughtlessness! What would I not give to have my father back again! This daily toil for bread, those hours of labor, prolonged often far into the night season—how cheerful would I be if they ministered to my father's comfort. Ah! if we had been loving and just to him, we might have had him still. But we were neither loving nor just. While he gathered with hard toil, we scattered. Daily we saw him go forth hurried to his business, and nightly we saw him come home exhausted; and we never put forth a hand to lighten his burdens; but, to gratify our idle and vain pleasures, laid new ones upon his stooping shoulders, until, at last, the cruel weight crushed him to the earth!

My father! Oh, my father! If grief and tearful repentance could have restored you to our broken circle, long since you would have returned to us. But tears and repentance are vain. The rest and peace of eternity is yours!

# XII.

## THE CHRISTIAN GENTLEMAN.

*IT* has been said that no man can be a gentleman who is not a Christian. We take the converse of this proposition, and say that no man can be a Christian who is not a gentleman.

There is something of a stir among the dry bones at this. A few eyes look at it in a rebuking way.

"Show me that in the Bible," says one in confident negation of our proposition.

"Ah, well, friend, we will take your case in illustration of our theme. You call yourself a Christian?"

"By God's mercy I do."

Answered with an assured manner, as if in no doubt as to your being a worthy bearer of that name.

"You seem to question my state of acceptance. Who made you a judge?"

Softly, friend. We do not like that gleam in your eyes. Perhaps we had better stop here. If you cannot bear the probe, let us put on the bandage again.

"I am not afraid of the probe, sir. Go on."

The name Christian includes all human perfection, does it not?

"Yes, and all God-like perfection in the human soul."

So we understand it. Now the fundamental doctrine of Christian life is this: —"As ye would that men should do unto you, do ye even so to them."

"Faith in Christ is fundamental," you answer.

Unless we believe in God, we cannot obey his precepts. The understanding must first assent, before the divine life can be brought into a conformity with divine laws. But we are not assuming theologic ground. It is the life to which we are looking. We said "The fundamental doctrine of Christian *life*."

"All doctrine has relation to life, and I contend for faith as fundamental."

We won't argue that point, for the reason that it would lead us away from the theme we are considering. We simply change the form of our proposition, and call it a leading doctrine of Christian life.

"So far I agree with you."

Then the way before us is unobstructed again. You asked us to show you authority in the Bible for saying that a man cannot be a Christian who is not a gentlemen. We point you to the Golden Rule. In that all laws of etiquette, so called, are included. It is the code of good breeding condensed to an axiom. Now it has so happened that our observation of you, friend objector, has been closer than may have been imagined. We have noted your outgoings and incomings on divers occasions; and we are sorry to say that you cannot be classed with the true gentleman.

"Sir!"

Gently! Gently! If a man may be a Christian, and not a gentleman at the same time, your case is not so bad. But to the testimony of fact. Let these witness for or against you. Let your own deeds approve or condemn. You are not afraid of judgment by the standard of your own conduct?

"Of course not."

And if we educe only well-remembered incidents, no offence will be

82

taken.

"Certainly not."

We go back, then, and repeat the law of true gentlemanly conduct. "As ye would that men should do unto you, do ye even so to them." You were at Stockbridge last summer?

"Yes."

And took supper at the hotel there, with a small company of strangers?

"Yes."

There was a dish of fine strawberries on the table, among the first of the season. You are fond of strawberries. They are your favorite fruit; and, as their rich fragrance came to your nostrils, you felt eager to taste them. So you counted the guests at the table, and measured the dish of strawberries with your eyes. Then you looked from face to face, and saw that all were strangers. Appetite might be indulged, and no one would know that it was *you*. The strawberries would certainly not go round, So you hurried down a cup of tea, and swallowed some toast quickly. Then you said to the waiter, "Bring me the strawberries." They were brought and set before you. And now, were you simply just in securing your share, if the number fell below a dozen berries? You were taking care of yourself; but in doing so, were not others' rights invaded. We shall see. There were eight persons at the table, two of them children. The dish held but little over a quart; of these nearly one-third were taken by you! Would a true gentleman have done that? You haven't thought of it since! We are sorry for you then. One of the children, who only got six berries, cried through half the evening from disappointment. And an invalid, whose blood would have gained life from the rich juice of the fruit, got none.

"It was a little selfish, I admit. But I am so fond of strawberries; and at hotels, you know, every one must take care of himself."

A true gentleman maintains his character under all circumstances, and a Christian, as a matter of course. A true gentleman defers to others. He takes so much pleasure in the enjoyment of others, that he denies himself in order to secure their gratification. Can a Christian do less and honor the name he bears?

"It wasn't right, I see."

Was it gentlemanly?

"No."

Christian?

"Perhaps not, strictly speaking."

In the gall of bitterness and the bonds of iniquity still, we fear, for all your profession. Christianity, as a system, must go deeper down into the heart than that. But we have begun with you, friend, and we will keep on. Perhaps you will see yourself a little differently by the time we are through. A poor mechanic, who had done some trifling work at your house, called, recently, with his little bill of three dollars and forty cents. You were talking with a customer, when this man came into your store and handed you his small account. You opened it with a slight frown on your brow. He had happened to come at a time when you felt yourself too much engaged to heed this trifling matter. How almost rudely you thrust the coarse, soiled piece of paper on which he had written his account back upon him, saying, "I can't attend to you now!" The poor man went out hurt and disappointed. Was that gentlemanly conduct? No, sir! Was it Christian? Look at the formula of Christian life. "As ye would that men should do unto you, do ye even so to them."

"He should have waited until I was at leisure," you answer. "When a man is engaged with a customer who buys at the rate of hundreds and thousands, he don't want paltry bills thrust into his face. He'll know better next time."

Have you settled the bill yet?

"No. He called day before yesterday, but couldn't give change for ten dollars."

Why haven't you sent him the trifling sum? He worked over half a day at your house, and your family have been more comfortable for what he did there ever since. He needs the money, for he is a poor man.

You half smile in our face at the suggestion, and say, "Merchants are not in the habit of troubling themselves to send all over the city to pay the little paltry bills of mechanics. If money is worth having, it is worth sending or calling for."

In thought, reverse your positions, and apply the rule for a Christian gentleman; remembering, at the same time, that God is no respecter of persons. In his eyes, the man's position is nothing—the quality of his life, everything.

A gentleman in *form*, according to the rules of good breeding, is one who treats everybody with kindness; who thinks of others' needs, pleasures and conveniences; and subordinates his own needs, pleasures and conveniences to theirs. He is mild, gentle, kind and courteous to all. A gentleman in *feeling* does all this from a principle of good-will; the Christian from a *law of spiritual life*. Now, a man may be a gentleman, in the common acceptation of the term, and yet not be a Christian; but we are very sure, that he cannot wave the gentleman and be a Christian.

You look at us more soberly. The truth of our words is taking hold of conviction. Shall we go on?

Do you not, in all public places, study your own comfort and convenience? You do not clearly understand the question! We'll make the matter plainer then:

Last evening you were at Concert Hall, with your wife and daughter. You went early, and secured good seats. Not three seats, simply, according to the needs of your party; but nearly five seats, for extra comfort. You managed it on the expansive principle. Well, the house was crowded. Compression and condensation went on all around you; but your party held its expanded position. A white-haired old man stood at the head of your seat, and looked down at the spaces between yourself, your wife and daughter; and though you knew it, you kept your eyes another way until he passed on. You were not going to be incommoded for any one. Then an old lady lingered there for a moment, and looked wistfully along the seat. Your daughter whispered, "Father, we can make room for her." And you answered: "Let her find another seat; I don't wish to be crowded." Thus repressing good impulses in your child, and teaching her to be selfish and unlady-like. The evening's entertainment began, and you sat quite at ease, for an hour and a half, while many were standing in the aisles. Sir, there was not even the gentleman in form here; much less the gentleman from naturally kind feelings. As to Christian principle, we will not take that into account. Do you remember what you said as you moved through the aisles to the door?

"No."

A friend remarked that he had been obliged to stand all the evening, and you replied:

"We had it comfortable enough. I always manage that, in public places."

He didn't understand all you meant; but, there is One who did.

How was it in the same place only a few nights previously? You went there alone, and happened to be late. The house was well filled in the upper portion, but thinly occupied below the centre. Now you are bound to have the best place, under all circumstances, if it can be obtained. But all the best seats were well filled; and to crowd more into them, would be to diminish the comfort of all. No matter. You saw a little space in one of the desirable seats, and into it you passed, against the remonstrance of looks, and even half uttered objections. A lady by your side, not in good health, was so crowded in consequence, and made so uncomfortable, that she could not listen with any satisfaction to the eloquent lecture she had come to hear.

We need say no more about your gentlemanly conduct in public places. Enough has been suggested to give you our full meaning.

Shall we go on? Do you call for other incidents in proof of our assumption? Shall we follow you into other walks of life?

"No."

Very well. And, now, to press the matter home: Do you, in the sight of that precept we have quoted, justify such conduct in a man who takes the name of Christian? It was not gentlemanly, in any right sense of the word; and not being so, can it be Christian?

"Perhaps not."

Assuredly not. And you may depend upon it, sir, that your profession, and faith, and church-going, and ordinance-observing, will not stand you in that day when the book of your life is opened in the presence of God. If there has been no genuine love of the neighbor—no self-abnegation—no self-denial for the good of others, all the rest will go for nothing, and you will pass over to abide forever with spirits of a like quality with your own.

Who made us your judge? We judge no man! But only point to the law of Christian life as given by God himself. If you wish to dwell with him, you must obey his laws; and obedience to these will make you nothing less than a Christian gentleman—that is, a gentleman in heart as well as in appearance.